Beautiful Mutants and
Swallowing Geography

Beautiful Mutants and *Swallowing Geography*

Two Early Novels

Deborah Levy

With an Introduction by Lauren Elkin

B L O O M S B U R Y

NEW YORK · LONDON · NEW DELHI · SYDNEY

Bloomsbury USA
An imprint of Bloomsbury Publishing Plc

1385 Broadway	50 Bedford Square
New York	London
NY 10018	WC1B 3DP
USA	UK

www.bloomsbury.com

BLOOMSBURY and the Diana logo are trademarks of Bloomsbury Publishing Plc

Beautiful Mutants first published by Jonathan Cape 1989
Swallowing Geography first published by Jonathan Cape 1993
This collection first published with the title *Early Levy* by Penguin Books 2014
This paperback edition published 2015

ISBN: TPB: 978-1-62040-675-5
ePub: 978-1-62040-676-2

LIBRARY OF CONGRESS CATALOGING-IN-PUBLICATION DATA HAS BEEN APPLIED FOR.

2 4 6 8 10 9 7 5 3 1

Typeset by Jouve (UK), Milton Keynes
Printed and bound in the U.S.A. by Thomson-Shore Inc., Dexter, Michigan

To find out more about our authors and books visit www.bloomsbury.com. Here you will find extracts,
author interviews, details of forthcoming events, and the option to sign up for our newsletters.

Bloomsbury books may be purchased for business or promotional use. For information on bulk purchases
please contact Macmillan Corporate and Premium Sales Department at specialmarkets@macmillan.com.

Contents

Introduction by Lauren Elkin   *vii*

BEAUTIFUL MUTANTS   I

SWALLOWING GEOGRAPHY   105

Introduction

Deborah Levy once wrote in an essay for *The Times* that when people ask her where she's from, she finds herself tempted 'to shrug nonchalantly and say: I was born in the forests of Bavaria and smuggled over the border in a hat box'.

A decade later, in her Man Booker shortlisted novel *Swimming Home* (2011), Levy bequeathed her Bavarian creation myth to her anti-hero Joe Jacobs, as well as the hard lesson she herself had been forced to learn. Joe was born Josef Nowogrodzki in western Poland in 1937, and his family emigrated to east London in 1942. As they fled, Joe recalls, 'His father had tried to melt him into a Polish forest when he was five years old. He knew he must leave no trace or trail of his existence because he must never find his way home. That was what his father had told him. You cannot come home. This was not something possible to know but he had to know it all the same.'

Occupying a tenuous place at the angle of the self and the world, Deborah Levy's writing – from her earliest short stories and novels to *Swimming Home* – shows that most of us are displaced, though we're trying not to be. To become aware of this is a gesture at self-honesty. Her first novel, *Beautiful Mutants* (1987), a Thatcher-era critique of Britain's docile submission to a results-oriented plutocracy, suggests that we're complicit in our alienation. 'This is the age of the migrant and the missile,' explains a character referred to only as The Poet, who works in a frozen-meat-packing factory. 'We have displaced our selves, banished our selves.' J.K., the main character in Levy's second novel, *Swallowing Geography* (1991), is described as 'the wanderer, bum, émigré, refugee, deportee, rambler, strolling player. Sometimes she would like to be a settler, but curiosity, grief and disaffection forbid it.' Levy's 1992 play, *The B-File*, is a choral work in six languages with one interpreter who translates the dialogue into the language where the play is being performed; at home everywhere, in every language, its main character is at home nowhere. Levy's unique achievement across the genres of theatre, poetry, novels and short stories is to make us aware of – and even to celebrate – the unhomely quality suffusing even the places we think we know best. Her work, especially early on, is a mythopoesis of exile.

Born in South Africa under apartheid in 1959, Levy moved to Britain with her family in 1968, when she was nine years old. While it's important not to lean too heavily on the role this reverse exile played in Levy's formation as a writer, being transplanted from one country to another greatly sensitized Levy to the power of voice. Immediately following her family's arrival in Britain, Levy was made aware of her South African accent at school, where no one could understand what she said, except a girl from Cork, Ireland. At home, Levy and her brother would play with different accents, imitating those they heard on television in *Steptoe and Son*, *On the Buses*, *The Liver Birds* and *Lost in Space*, delighting in the varied treatments and deformations of vowels, unable, at that age, to discern class through speech. Our voices, Levy learned, both cover up and betray who we really are. Our hesitations and our stammerings are a means of not letting through something that we don't want to say; they are symptoms of what's really eating us. That is part of Levy's achievement in *Swimming Home*: she produced a novelistic, storytelling language out of her characters' linguistic insufficiencies; they both fail and succeed in conveying their urgencies, their worries, their fears. An apprenticeship in the theatre crystallized this preoccupation with voice: Levy studied playwriting at Dartington College of Arts, and soon after found acclaim writing for the Royal Shakespeare Company. The polyphony of the theatre, and its marriage of voice, body and story, carries through into her early prose work.

Beautiful Mutants and *Swallowing Geography* are a trial run for the strategies Levy would employ later; in particular, they show her gearing up to write *The Unloved* (1994), her first long narrative work. The early novels are saturated with the intensity of an old photo of the author taken during the era: half frowning, half pouting, cheekbones sharp, hair done up in a punk tulle bow, cigarette held between thumb and forefinger. We can almost see her going home to pore over Angela Carter and Kathy Acker, Antonin Artaud and Jean Genet; we can almost hear in the background Poly Styrene, Siouxsie Sioux, Debbie Harry, Patti Smith and Nina Hagen. Reading the novels, other portraits emerge: the young artist as sensitive instrument, registering the everyday atrocities imposed by an unfeeling ruling class; the apprentice writing into the tradition (or anti-tradition) of the literary avant-garde; the playwright straying from the theatre, revelling in what can be done on the page, instead of the stage.

Beautiful Mutants was published two years before the Berlin Wall came down; its central character is Lapinski, a young woman in exile from Moscow, who is surrounded by a cast of quasi-allegorical figures. With a detached wryness reminiscent of Djuna Barnes's *Nightwood*, Levy's misfits narrate the novel in turns: The Poet, the Anorexic Anarchist, The Banker, who becomes so empowered by capitalism she feels invincible enough to set fire to London Zoo. (Poor giraffe, poor elephants.) Even in this scorched landscape, Levy is a startlingly funny writer, with an inbuilt sense of the absurd, a preference for surrealism over realism. This is not incompatible with the seriousness of her concerns; these more fragmented early works display a Rabelaisian belief in the subversive power of laughter. There is Lapinski's neighbour, who calls her a 'shameless cunt' because she never has the same accent from one day to the next ('it changes like the English weather') and because she shows disdain towards his plastic love dolly. There is also a talking llama, who Lapinski's lover turns to for advice on how to make his life meaningful. The llama counsels: 'Go into international finance, become a dynamic sales manufacturer in a high-growth computer company, become a senior sales consultant [. . .] OH SLUTTY SON be result-motivated!' Levy sketches a society which marches zombie-like through a world built by capitalist interests: 'Outside, on the high street, people put bits of plastic into a brick wall and in return get money. They carry their personal number around with them, in their sleep, during meals, love play, in swimming baths and offices.' As the people become machine-like, the machines become people-like: 'The computer in the wall is hot, like the forehead of a person with a fever, burning into the bricks and mortar of Europe.' 'Tomorrow is always another day,' reasons Lapinski's neighbour, 'because you can always buy something.' Lapinski tries to jolt her neighbour out of his passive acceptance that spending equals being, but her intervention leaves him befuddled. 'I tell [Lapinski] to write down everything she spends in a little book so she'll know where she is,' he explains. 'She says she does write everything down but she still doesn't know where she is and where do I think I am?'

In *Swallowing Geography*, Levy's sense of the absurd has become more elegiac. J.K. – 'Europe's eerie child' – no longer knows who she is or where she's from. She dreams of a 'white "Chinese" horse on her hotel wall' who whispers at her:

We return to homelands and find they are a hallucination. We return to our mothers and fathers and find they are not the people we thought they were. We return to our street and find it has been re-named. We return to our cities and find they have been re-built. We return to our lovers and find they are elsewhere even when they lie in our bed [. . .] The redemptive homeland, she is a joker, she runs away bells ringing on her toes, you chase her at your peril because she will appear disguised as something else and you will be chasing her all your life.

As in *Beautiful Mutants*, the thematic sense of displacement and dislocation replicates at the level of the sentence, as strange juxtapositions join up like body parts at odd angles. *Swallowing Geography* gives us disparate characters standing close together in a frame, desiring without understanding each other. J.K. likes it that way: she feels protected by mystery. But her lovers long to minimize this distance; one wants her to take off her shoes so he can know her better, another wants to impregnate her to tie her down. For J.K., to be known is to be colonized, neutralized, immobilized. 'To name someone,' Levy writes, 'is to give them a country. To give them a country is to give them an address. To give them an address is to give them a home.' The claims we place on each other, and on the world around us, are forever multiplying, keeping pace with our instinctive need to possess, and to locate. Around J.K. and her lovers and friends, the jumble of the world is constantly in flux even against these attempts to fix its outlines. Borders are constantly redrawn – the novel registers everything from the reshaping of the former Soviet Union and the partitioning of London into two new telephone codes, 'Central and Suburban', to the reorganization of a front room – and the novel's characters must unhinge themselves from fear of change and recommit to the 'matter-of-factness' of daily life in the 'cities we know best'.

The fervent imagery and sweeping ambition of the two novels are the mark of a young writer who is learning to harness her energies; they have a distinct shimmer that is Levy through and through, and show her determination to employ what she learned from Don DeLillo's *White Noise* (1985): 'a new poetics to describe postmodern life'. Articulating this is the basis of the contract Levy discerns between reader and writer. 'We live through the same historical events, and the same Pepsi ads,' she wrote in the *Independent* in 1998. 'Writers and readers, nervously sharing this all too fluid world, circle each other to find out what the hell is going on.'

– Lauren Elkin

Beautiful Mutants

My mother was the ice-skating champion of Moscow. She danced, glided, whirled on blades of steel, pregnant with me, warm in her womb even though I was on ice. She said I was conceived on the marble slab of a war memorial, both she and my father in their Sunday best; I came into being on a pile of corpses in the bitter snows of mid-winter. Afterwards they bought themselves a cone full of *ponchiki*, doughnuts dripping with fat and sprinkled with powdered sugar, and ate them outside the Kursk railway station, suddenly shy of the passion that had made them search for each other so urgently under all those clothes. On my fifth birthday, my father stole a goose. He stuffed it into the pocket of his heavy overcoat and whizzed off on his motorbike, trying to stop it from flying away with his knees. We ate it that evening, and as I put the first forkful into my mouth he tickled me under the chin and said, 'This does not exist, understand?' I did not understand at the time, especially as my mother stuffed a pillow full of the feathers for me, and soaked the few left over in red vegetable dye to sew on to the skirt of her skating costume.

When my parents died, I was sent to the West at the age of twelve by my grandmother, survivor of many a pogrom and collector of coffee lace handkerchiefs. She said it was for the best, but I think she just wanted to enjoy her old age without the burden of yet another child to look after. I was to stay with a distant uncle in London. When I asked my grandmother why he had left Russia she whispered, 'Because he is faithless' and busied herself wrapping little parcels of spiced meat from Georgia for me to take on the ship. Her letters were written on torn sheets of brown paper, three lines long and usually the same three lines in a different order; short of breath as always.

In London, where women were rumoured to swim in fountains dressed in leopard-skin bikinis, I unpacked my few clothes, books, photographs, parcels of meat, and wept into the handkerchief my grandmother had pressed into my hand, embroidered in one scarlet thread with my name . . . L.A.P.I.N.S.K.I.

The Poet smells of cashew nuts and cologne. She drinks tea from a transparent cup of cheap rose-coloured glass and says, 'This is the age of the migrant and the missile, Lapinski. In some ways you could say our time has come.' She laughs and her gold teeth rattle. Her hands are raw from making frozen hamburgers which is her job. Every morning a coach takes The Poet and other workers to an industrial estate on the outskirts of the city, clutching bags full of shoes to change into, hand-creams and hairnets. 'Exile is a state of mind.' She taps her wide forehead.

Tonight I will cook for The Poet a bitter, aromatic stew my grandmother taught me to make when I was a child, a dish for hunters with guns and moustaches who like to track small animals across the snow. She watches me put cabbage, rabbit, funghi, lilac, mushrooms, prunes, honey, red wine, salt and peppercorns into a pot.

'We on the meatbelt, Lapinski, blood under our fingernails, are not in a factory on the edge of the motorway, we are somewhere quite different. We are decorating our bedrooms, cleaning the house, making up conversations that will probably never be spoken, on a mountain, writing a book, trying out a new mascara, making plans for children, or for the future which is one day, at most one week, ahead. I myself am alone on the shores of the Black Sea coast or sitting under a fig tree in the paradise of Adam and Eve. If you were to count the thousands of miles between us as machines hum and our fingers linger on control buttons, you could cover the universe. We take ourselves through borders of every kind and carry no passport.

'I know women who work in their sleep and wake when the bell goes, women who sing lullabies, laments and pop songs in time with the machine, women who unknown to themselves make sculptures from meat, the burgers take on the shape of their thoughts; I have seen great pyramids of thought sail across stainless steel into another life.

'I have a good friend on the meatbelt, Lapinski, her name is Martha and she has soft white hands. In the tea-break she can hear the sea because she wears earrings made from shells and she swallows two spoonfuls of a thick expectorant for her cough every day – her lungs growl and she is often breathless. Sometimes she says she can see an image of her own face in the meatmound and who am I, Lapinski, to disagree? You will remember that when Saint Veronica met Jesus, she paused to wipe the sweat off his face and discovered that his image was for ever after imprinted on the cloth? I think of Martha as a modern saint because her visions have helped her not be defeated by her circumstances. Saint Martha paints her fingernails the colour of Portuguese oranges, defying the cardboard pallor of meatbelt life. We have displaced our selves, banished our selves. We are in exile.'

The sulphurous light of the city glows on The Poet's fingertips. She has carried sacks of tea on her head through plantations of hazelnut and tobacco in the burning late morning sun. At five she sold gum and matches in Eastern villages. At seventeen she cut off her beautiful hair and unlike Samson found strength in the birth of her strong neck. In the slum cities of Northern Europe she lost her health. Coffee cups in greasy cafés offered her dark and difficult visions. And then she lost her mind. She lost her self in the architectural, rational, cultural, political, anatomical structures of Northern European cities and began to vibrate with confusion and pain. She turned inwards and lay in the damp crease of her pillow for twenty-eight days and nights. The sound of police sirens replaced the song of lottery callers, chestnut sellers, canaries and laughter. In her dreams she became a stone, eroded and reshaped by the tides, on the telephone she tried to talk to her mother but found she no longer had a language they both understood.

She held on to the bloody threads of each day, invisible with hundreds of other foreign workers, the brown underbelly of the city, some broken, some brave, but always dreaming, writing letters home, thinking of loved ones, hoping for better times. She survived on odd jobs, cleaning, sewing in sweat shops, looking after other women's children. It was at this time that The Poet mistressed the skill of metamorphosis. She learnt she had to become many selves in order to survive. Through observation, study and meditation she taught herself to change from one self to another, from one state to another. If she had no identity she would have many identities; she learnt she was engaged in a war and saw how those who are confused and in pain, or have some secret sorrow of their own, bring out an instinct in others who refuse to acknowledge the possibility of this pain in themselves, to crush, humiliate and hurt. The Poet refused to be crushed.

She waited for the storm inside her to be over. And when it was, in the parts that were torn, she planted sunflowers. She finished her cleaning, bought bread and dates, sat on benches in city parks looking at children scuff their knees in cement.

Chewing the white unbleached flour of the bread she liked best, she decided that the word justice did not mean law and order, and the word opportunity did not mean organized human misery. And as she swallowed the bread she also swallowed the humility of being a confused human being; devoted herself obsessively to understanding her condition and thus the condition of others. 'Lapinski,' she croaks, eating an iced bun, for she is no exotic, 'I have been a foolish casualty, a bitten fruit.'

Tears trickle down the veins of her brown arm.
In her eyes, whole continents seem to flicker.

It is true she turns her male lovers into swine.
It is true she rides over corn and heads of grasses.
These are merely images.
She is a poet.

'Y'know I love you Y'know I love you Y'know I love you.' It is a woman's voice, breathless and monotonous, and cutting through her, an angry man shouting 'I don't know, I don't know.' I run upstairs and bang on the door with both fists, 'Y'know I love you' getting louder as I bang again. The man who lives there opens the door, first a little and then wider, a little pot of pink yoghurt clasped to his chest. 'Hello, Lapinski,' he says. We stare at each other and all the time, she, the woman is saying 'Y'know I love you Y'know I love you Y'know I love you.' He smiles, 'She comes in three sizes,' and points to a doll, five foot long, lying on the floor in front of the flickering television, yellow plastic skin, black hair and slanting eyes. 'Just taming the savage,' he says.

As I turn to go he shouts, 'Lapinski, don't thump on my door again you cunt . . . I'm relaxing with a strawberry yoghurt. Do you know my dolly can talk? She's moved in with me and she only says nice things.' He points with his teaspoon to the O of her dead talking mouth.

The sound of a piano playing in some hidden part of the city drifts ghost-like through the walls. A strange, ecstatic sound; fragile and triumphant and full of bones. When The Poet throws back her head and roars with laughter, my cat stares into her mouth with wonder. 'Today I saw a band of clowns in the street, banging drums, dancing, red noses and baggy checked trousers. They were shouting 'Join the community church . . . join today . . . Jesus enjoyed a good joke . . . Jesus liked to laugh too,' and they gave out free balloons to passers-by who were desperate to laugh and so they did because if you see a red nose you must laugh and be happy. I don't think Jesus was so begging that he wore a red nose in the desert in case a passing nomad needed cheering up?'

We have finished our stew and I am polishing The Poet's boots. She has only one pair and they have to last. My cat loves The Poet.

They watch fat moths circle the lamp and when I hear bird noises I don't know which of the two is making them. They have long conversations I don't understand. I pass her the gleaming boots – my father taught me to polish my school shoes every morning in the special way an icon maker from Yalta taught him. The Poet grudgingly admires her boots (the icon maker was a vain man and made sure the tricks he passed on would be admired), wraps a shawl around her shoulders, pins it with a glistening brooch. 'I'll be off, Lapinski, I can see from that glint in your bleary eyes you want to light your second cigar of the evening and summon a few demons. Oh don't deny it . . . don't deny it . . . like all people who feel uncomfortable in an uncomfortable world you want to make a map. Well let me tell you it is difficult to make a map in splintered times when whole worlds and histories collide.' She kisses me on the cheek and says goodbye to my cat with her eyes, which are turquoise tonight. 'When I first met you, Lapinski, you were attempting to brew vodka from peach stones . . .' Small and bright and certain against the night sky, she walks in the direction of the zoo. As she turns the corner, she looks like a beast of burden. A llama. An animal that survives in harsh climates. Hunted for meat, milk, wool, dung.

Rain falls from a luminous sky on the broken wing of a Chinese umbrella, and under it a woman walks through the heart of London, with fast little steps in the direction of the hospital. She can hear voices, maybe from the cocktail bar where a young entrepreneur in sunglasses talks feverishly, breath quickening like an eroticized mercenary planning a raid, pointing to his 'joybox', a

Ferrari parked outside. She says to the boy leaning against the wall, little ivory skull glued to the toe of his shoe, 'It's happy hour and my friend is dying. I have to find the hospital.' He gives her a cigarette which she lights, balancing her broken umbrella

> *On your old breast, dear*
> *My permed head I'll rest, dear*

wipes the rain out of her eyes and stares into his with an expression he cannot meet. 'We must treat the dying like kings you know.' She looks into the window of the bar where two waiters, blond hair gelled and parted immaculately in the middle, serve pink champagne and langoustines. They glide from table to table carrying pecan pie and crème caramel on the dip of their wrists, the backs of their long necks shaved in symmetrical sculptures. The blonder waiter gives a customer a small pair of metal pliers to crack the claws of his lobster. The woman looks at the boy again, smiles a ravishing smile, adjusts the lemon silk of her best suit and says, 'I've always been partial to lobster myself.' She crosses the road and, blinded by the rain, trips over a pigeon-coloured blanket that turns out to be a man sleeping rough on the pavement.

Lapinski is a shameless cunt. I don't know what accent she's wearing today because it changes like the English weather, but I do know she hates my plastic love dolly and can't stand me either. She makes me feel weird under my suit but when I told her she made me feel weird she said I probably feel weird anyway. Her eyes gore into my ribs and crack them just when I think I've impressed her.

When she comes upstairs to whine at me about my lifestyle I have to spray my flat with a floral aerosol because she stinks. I think it's because she seals the soles of her flat brown shoes with donkey dung – or so she says – but then she told me she washes her hair in it too because it's a natural conditioner and brings out her chestnut highlights. I put newspaper down when she walks in just in case there's some truth in it. Sometimes she brings me frozen hamburgers some mate gives to her; I think she rubs garlic under her fingernails – I have to rush to the fridge, grab a beer and gargle with it to get a hold on things. Don't ever expect a simple answer to a simple question from Lapinski. She doesn't know how to talk straight. If you ask her if she likes dogs (I have a terrier called Duke) she says 'only curried' and then she pats

Duke and strokes his ears and he falls in love with the cunt and whimpers when she leaves. She's got a job cooking in a café for foreign people and she's always broke. I tell her to write down everything she spends in a little book so she'll know where she is. She says she does write everything down but she still doesn't know where she is and where do I think I am?

My dad was the last blacksmith in our town and he was a social-ist; he worked eleven hours a day, as a welder. When I was young my mother could never make ends meet and had to ask the butcher for bones for the dog – and then make us broth with them. My father wrote a song called 'Bones for the Dog', it came to him while he was sweating in the dark with fire and metal. He sang it in the pub dressed in a suit the colour of granite. Well I don't want to be a stone – there's too much blood in it, too many late night tearful conversations about how to get by in it – too many fucking dog bones in it. Singing in the pub won't buy me a future. I prefer the wine bar. Working in the city, so long as your head looks like an arse (all us guys went bald this year), so long as you're deliver-ing to target, the only thing that will get you sacked is being too honest – or possibly a full head of hair. When I go back to see my mum I sometimes catch her looking at me as if I am a complete stranger; her eyes settle on my suit like a half-starved fly – I feel stripped in front of her large stupid body, shuffle about the house trying to find words that will make her like me. She gave me some runner-beans from the garden and I threw them out of the win-dow on the motorway.

I have bought myself a new toy. It's called The Revenger – a compact disc that I slip into the dashboard of my Nissan whenever

I feel like relaxing. When you press the button you hear the sound of machine-gun fire as you crawl from red light to red light in the rush hour. Yesterday I had the gun belting out and saw a tart waiting on the kerb. Red fishnet tights and blonde ponytail; she made me tremble so I wound down the window. She looked beautifully shocked, it wiped the snarl off her slutty lips. I wanted her lips. She ran away – did she really think I'd fill her lovely soft belly with bullets? I followed her for half a mile down the road and when I caught up with her fishy legs said, 'What's your name?'

'Tremor.'

'Well Tremor, you make me tremble, how about a massage?'

The thought of a massage while listening to The Revenger sort of appealed. Like perfume in the trenches, or clean white satin under the rags of a whore in Tokyo where I sometimes do business. We had good sex on the back seat, with the engine running so I could keep the machine-gun firing. Her red tights lay like a puddle of blood on the floor.

She said I hurt her, I said I pay to hurt her. I don't like them with stretch marks on their stomachs – it's a turn-off to think of tarts as mothers. When she put the money in her handbag I saw she had a little plastic duck in it, the sort babies float in their bath. The next morning her hair was all over the seat cover.

Lapinski's cat is almost as vile as she is. She calls it, how do you say it, K.R.U.P.S.K.A.Y.A. No wonder he's nearly as far gone as his mistress. I think Bill is a reasonable name for a tom. The other day that cunt of a cat bit my ear. I kicked it down the stairs and bathed my lughole with Dettol but I think it's got infected. Lapinski says it was infected anyway – whaat? She talks rubbish all night with her friends and smokes little Cuban cigars – they arrive for her every month in the post in a little wooden box. Her breath made me cry when she peered into my ear and of course she told me I was crying anyway. Why isn't she crying? Her cardigan's got holes in the elbow and she has to walk home because she often doesn't have the bus-fare. Yesterday I saw her skipping over the lines of the pavement.

Maybe it's the Muzak coming in through the window, someone playing the piano: tonight I feel a bit down. The doctor has given me some pale pink pills, which was thoughtful of him because they match my tie.

I'll tell you something about Lapinski. When she gets a gas bill, she writes all over it with a thick black felt-tip, THIS DOES NOT EXIST, and sends it to the gas board. Her eyebrows meet in the middle.

Dear Lapinski,

*In the mellow autumnal breeze I had a farcical chase after
your lipstuck Rizla which got blown about and nearly lost. But
I'm going to save it until we are next alone when I shall offer it
to you wrapped around something appropriately aphrodisiacal.*

Freddie

I have summoned my first love demon and he has answered my
call. This is no act of the supernatural, more to do with the art of
suggestion. I kissed the transparent skin of a Rizla, thinking of the
cold wars we raged on each other's skin, tucked it behind Krupskaya's
ear and watched her disappear into the night. She is the Messenger of
Broken Dreams. These errands keep her fit and sleek. I journeyed
from the Iron Curtain to the black Venetian blinds of a Western
man's bedroom, and learnt love alone will not smash the atom.

We are walking on damp cement. Hand in hand. I wear a dazzling
emerald dress. He tells me every time he makes an inspired brush-
stroke on canvas he hears the voice of Salvador Dalì whisper *'Olé!'*

and last night, which he spent without me, he was upset not to find three snails on his hot-water bottle. At his studio we eat rice with red hot pepper. 'I am hopeful for that painting there . . .' He points to a large canvas propped up against the wall '. . . because every-one loves a butterfly and it is full of butterflies.' His long lidded eyes settle on my body like the Inquisition. Light shines on his short corn-stubble hair, his apricot body and thick lips. 'You are my butterfly,' he says, stroking the thin emerald cloth on my breast. His fingers slip under under my dress and all the time the sun is shining on him. I begin to sting and smart. The red hot pepper on his fingers and the possibility of love, yearned and dreamt for, the possibility of great love for ever and ever two inches away from my roaring heart.

In a caravan surrounded by geese and nettles, we eat a selection of cheeses. Goat, cow, sheep. We drink red wine. I am thinking this is the Last Supper because Freddie has been sleeping with another woman and I am upset. He bought her a bottle of lime pickle which seems to me a very intimate thing to do; he knows what she likes to taste. Just as my mother and father slipped away from me in a tram crash on a bridge where, months after their death, I'd stand looking down at the water below and imagine I could see them floating – a shoe, my mother's green skirt, my father's heavy overcoat – floating down and away from me, so I feel his love slipping away from me, and into her. I want him to declare his love so I can give him mine; instead he looks out hungrily, loots other sexual scenarios, comes to me changed, and fumbling and shy we have to find where we last left off, who we were before. Now he strokes my neck while geese run about the field and wind rocks the caravan. It is late autumn and loss is in the air; I am too familiar with its sensation; it haunts me in dreams and at unexpected moments, brushing my hair or waiting for a bus. He says, 'Where'd ya lose your heart?' I look down and see the gold heart I wear on a chain round my neck has fallen off. I search the floor of the caravan, hand clutching the place my heart once was, my very very precious heart, given to me by my grandmother that day she pressed the handkerchief into my hand. He comments on the blue black colours in my hair, yawns, smiles, stretches, says, 'You know, a lot of fashionable and influential image-makers would say that gold heart is naff. You have nothing to lose but your chain.'

On the beach we look at each other through a hole in a stone. He sucks all the green from my eye. He is a reader of colour, texture, signs, of the space between things, of light and dark and gesture. He stands outside himself and observes. He is interested in sensation. He is sensual. He admires me. I say, 'When I was twelve and arrived in the West, I drank Coke through a blue straw and thought it would make me free and if everyone in East Germany could drink it too the wall would come down, so someone said, Why not chip off a bit of the wall, drop it into a glass of Coke and see if it dissolves overnight?' He likes bizarre juxtapositions and contrives them in his paintings, his love play, his clothes, his conversation. I love him but try not to. He makes me cry. He is bewildered. He stands outside my tears, and watches them in relation to the window frame and straw chair.

On the beach we stare at each other through a hole in a stone. We are in love but we are scared and when we look away, he sings

*In a fishing boat
when the light turned blue
you burgled me
and I burgled you*

We are East and West looting each other.

We hang a washing-line across the room. It is draped with feathers and flowers and sheep bones found on walks, the insides of clocks and TV sets. It is the Berlin Wall. We declare an uneasy peace. War is more sexy. We are afraid to make peace. We sharpen our weapons. We pride ourselves on our weapons. If we were to make a peace treaty, to disarm, we would have to come to the conference table naked and we are afraid of our nakedness. He falls in love with someone else to punish me.

I am thinking of his mother. How she once told me she was merely alone and not abandoned. He says, 'You are my butterfly.' I am thinking of his father. How in the war he brought his girl-friend home to live in his wife's house and how she, who is merely alone and not abandoned, washed her husband's girlfriend's clothes in the bath. Peering at the labels. Good clothes. And how his father (after he had abandoned his wife) got a disease that made him shake so severely he could no longer play cricket in his immaculate whites on England's green killing fields. He says, 'I have the body of Jesus Christ and the soul of Lenin. Are you going to crucify me then with the curl of your lips?' No I am not. I am going to abandon you. He cleans his paintbrush with a rag, feeling abandoned and exhilarated.

*

'In fact, Lapinski,' says Freddie, in his mellow autumnal back-yard, waving the lipstuck Rizla, 'dressed as you are in creams and blues you look like a gentle bruise.

'Forgive me I am shaking. there are roots poking through the walls of my flat, through the floor and through the ceiling, and I thought of you because you always said you had no roots. Perhaps you dropped a few seeds all those years ago. Yesterday, Lapinski, I stole a statue of Freud from a London park and carried him home. And I danced for him, swinging my hips, until I became paralysed. First my neck, but that was okay, it was interesting, I could still move the rest of my body. Then my arms froze in a great O shape above my head, wrists turned in on themselves, but my legs still danced on. I explored the family trees in my joints, muscles, bones, and then I became totally paralysed . . . statue-like in front of the statue Freud. He watched me and then he spoke, asked for cocaine, books, a cigar, a florentine from a Viennese pâtisserie. I asked him whether my paralysis was real or a state of mind, but he was silent and staring. Staring at my penis, so I got an erection, and that became frozen too, which is to say, Lapinski, what am I to do with this lipstuck Rizla? Am I to attempt trans-meditational coitus with you – Lapinski who dropped her seed somewhere in me, like the male fish who carries eggs in his mouth?

'Lapinski, I have desires I don't understand. I dreamt I made women do things they didn't want to do, made them squeal with pain and ecstasy, tied them up and beat them and fucked them in their most secret places. I woke up sweating, it was terrible and wonderful, and as women walked the streets on the way to buy milk or cigarettes I thought . . . it could be her, she's the one. I will take her back to my chamber of ferocious fumbling, my chamber of a hundred hidden orifices and she will enjoy it. I will make her queen and I will be king. Lapinski, I am not a brute . . . I do not have steel tips on my boots . . . I want you to be strong and brave and beautiful but I also want to crush you . . . want you to have your own will and desires but I also want to tame and domesticate you. I want you to want me but I don't want you. Lapinski, I have had many lovers but as soon as they want me I don't want them either. Remember when I deserted you and went off with the woman who grew lilies on her balcony, and the woman with the fake cherries pinned to the ribbon of her straw hat, and the woman with the yellow kid gloves, and the woman with the ideas, and the woman whose nipples I sucked till the sun disappeared for ever, and the woman who kept Valium in her sugar tin, and the woman reading alone in the apple orchard, and the woman who varnished boats in Marseille, and the woman who ate and ate and then sicked up in washing-up bowls, and the woman who taught her children how to make necklaces from pistachio nuts, and the woman who collected lizards, and the woman who cooked curries that made me hallucinate. Well, Lapinski, they were ponds, ponds to drown everything I do not want to feel. As soon as I start to feel something I find another pond. I am trying to confess, Lapinski, you have flown away from me but I have pinned you on to my canvas and everyone loves butterflies so you might have brought me luck in the marketplace. My woman from somewhere else. Open your wings and kiss me here . . . here . . . here . . . land on me there, I can't sleep without you fluttering by my side and, anyway, one day I will be famous and I will buy you three villas in three different countries and you will have a cook and a driver and someone to iron your emerald dress but for now I want to fill myself up with your lips, with moments that give me reason to continue . . . but I don't know where to find them.'

He is shaking. Shaking. Freddie is breaking down. He weeps and laughs at the same time. He carries the scent of a thousand women in his armpits, his tears are the jewels they took off, or put on, for him, he is shaking just like his father shook before him, shaking into the moon, lipstuck Rizla spiked on his forefinger. Who will put him together again?

'Lapinski.'

'Yes?'

'I am going to break into the zoo.'

He disappears in the direction of the zoo, where sometimes, at night, wolves can be heard howling through the bars of their cage. I once heard a man howl just like a wolf except he was standing in a phone box in Streatham.

It is the age of the Great Howl.

No woman has ever fallen in love with me.

Last year I fell for a policewoman called Chloe but in the end she married her personal trainer, a man called Rod (born in Brazil) who always carried boxing gloves and pads in his holdall so his clients could have a go at him any time they had a spare hour. I liked Chloe's uniform and the streaks in her hair and the way she rode her horse. And she was bloody brave. She restrained (at her leisure) some fucker who sold her a dodgy endowment policy – by the time her leisure was over his teeth were no longer in his mouth. Last time I saw her, before she got engaged to Rod, she told me they were training her up to drive a tank. I said, 'Is there going to be a coup then?' but the tank thing was about her being posted to Wales where the miners were on strike and she was going to sort them out – that was what they were all going to do at her station, sort out the miners. She said she liked sorting things out if it paid her mortgage – and then she winked at me. I reckoned I had met the woman of my dreams. I could hear myself saying, do this and this and this and do it harder and she replying yes yes yes oh yes oh yes yes yes – but that will never happen because I don't need sorting out.

Last Sunday I went to a pub on the borders of West Sussex with two guys from the office. We had roast chicken with all the trimmings that made this country great and we warmed our selves by the coal fire. I gave my apple crumble to Duke who was causing trouble because I'd tied him up outside and he doesn't like the wind. And then I had this dream that I was dead and someone had put a lump of coal in my mouth, like a pig with an apple in its gob. For the last three nights I've heard Lapinski crying through the early hours. I don't know what's happened and I don't like to ask because she might tell me. Her cat *Krupskaya* made a jump for Duke yesterday. Duke gets annoyed and tries to bite her head off. So what does *Krup* do? Run away? Not on your life. She jumps on top of his back and sticks there like a pot of glue. Duke begins to run about in circles and whine so I have to call Lapinski up. She stomps in, leaving mud, or donkey dung, all over my carpet so I have a go despite the fact her eyes are red and swollen. She told me I should take Duke out for a walk more often – and then she starts to unstick Krup by offering her the slab of pâté I had just bought from the deli. Duke licked her horrible hands and wanted to go home with her but I gave him the look Chloe taught me and he fell into line. Another thing. My mother's father was a miner.

It is by the mirror, where I practise narcissism, that I summon my second demon. For it is she who wrote me letters of love, written backwards so I had to read them through the looking glass. 'Backwards letters are my escape,' she said.

She is fifteen years old, voluptuous, ribbons and flowers and bits of old lace tangled in her mane of blonde hair; she wears Mexican smocks embroidered with silken greens on crisp white cotton, lips shining, a pot of gloss always at hand so that crumbs stick to her lips. She is full of fury and smells of roses.

'This, Lapinski, is my family.' She points to each of them: '. . . This is my father who has forgotten how to love; this is my mother who has forgotten how to think; these are my sisters who will all go into the wine trade . . . and this . . .' she bursts into tears '. . . is my life.' The aroma of freshly ground coffee lingers about the house.

She is on holiday with her business tycoon daddy and her sisters. An oily pensive anchovy on the beach, ashamed of her large breasts and little broken fingernails, surrounded by her father's girlfriends, film cronies, American and English exiles, models, villa owners, local boutique owners and hangers-on, she feels flawed. They swim, eat, arrange barbecues, play backgammon, strip poker, have massages, manicures, sunbathe, swap gossip. She watches them, her mouth tingling with ulcers.

Her fists beat the burning sand.
  'I will escape,' she writes.

A glamorous model drapes her long tanned legs over the business tycoon's lap. Gemma stares sulkily at her daddy, who playfully slaps the bottom of the model. The model turns to Gemma. 'We're being nice to each other because I'm filming in the Caribbean soon and we won't see other for too long.' She kisses the tycoon's ears. 'I am a very busy woman, Gemma,' she smiles. Gemma snaps her book shut, and stands up, scattering sand and suntan lotions. '*Your very busy life and very empty mind are what I want to escape from.*' The truth is she doesn't really know what it is she wants to escape from.

Gemma, who will later become The Banker, is seventeen years old; she gives me her cast-offs and I go home to my uncle's with carrier bags stuffed full of shoes and dresses, and Charles of the Ritz lipsticks. Years later, Freddie, who has a liking for silks and cashmeres, will run his hands slowly down my body, in Gemma's clothes, exploring buttonholes and pleats and the cut of a sleeve. And years later I will look into the mirror and see his tongue inside Gemma's mouth as they writhe about in a bed of flames.
  Gemma stamps the floor with her high heels. We fight about money and class and privilege. She cries prettily, passionately,

stops, reads me my horoscope, squeals and squeaks 'Eeeeeeeeeek,' calls me a 'meanie', flicks through magazines, works for hours in the school library. She is brilliant and sharp, asks teachers a hundred questions they cannot answer, shouts in exasperation. She loves me, she says, and asks me to trim her hair with a little pair of blunt scissors. She doesn't like pubs because they are full of 'sad people'. She is afraid of poor people.

After school she buys me a hot chocolate at the bus station. I sip it very slowly and then she finishes it off for me, a chocolate moustache on her immaculate face, waving goodbye and blowing kisses.

The morning after she has finished her Oxbridge entry exams, we sit on a bench eating monkey nuts, feeding pigeons with the shells. Her fingers are covered in ink and all the flowers have fallen out of her hair.

At Oxford, Gemma fluffs her hair, glosses her lips and tells a swarthy Italian economist at a cheese and wine party that she despises her hall full of simpering ninnies running baths of Avon bubbles and cooking little pans of sensible soup. 'They're so prim.' He smiles, offering her sausage on a stick. She eats it fast, and guiltily. 'Even a sedate patch of *blue* on the eyelids is considered fast.' He doesn't know what she's talking about, but her cleavage is exciting and she displays it with pride. His suit is dull but well cut, his white shirt starched. She says, closing her eyes and giggling inside, 'I like men in suits.'

Gemma invites him back to her room for water. She drinks pints and pints of it a day because she read in one of her glossy magazines it will make her thin. She shows him a picture of me, in a polka-dot dress. 'This is my friend Lapinski. Don't you think she looks like Sofia Loren?' The economist nods (liar), fiddling with his cufflinks. 'When I was fifteen I escaped into Lapinski's arms. I love her passionately.' The Italian economist leaves immediately. Tomorrow she will dine with a Panamanian economist she met in a Marx lecture. Apparently he is very rich and owns a plantation.

The Panamanian economist and Gemma fondle each other in her single bed. He cups her face in his hands, stares into her eyes, asks her to put some ice on his penis.

'Ice?'

'Yes pleeeeeeeeeease.'

But the future Banker is intrepid and creeps to the communal kitchens where she finds one of the simpering ninnies brewing cocoa in her nightdress.

'Hello Gemma,' she blinks dozily.

'I'm looking for ice.'

'Ice?'

'I'm very hot.'

They yank out a large jagged slab of ice from the freezer and Gemma trots back to her economist trailing her kimono on the corridor floor.

'Tra la la tra la la la la.'

She throws it on to his penis and, still singing, climbs on top of him.

'Aaaaaaaaaaah.' He comes immediately. The smell of fish fills the room. Wafts between them. It reminds the Panamanian economist of the fish markets in his home town, flies swarming around piles of roe and guts, and the jokes told by men about the whores they'd had the night before. Both attribute the smell to themselves and feel humiliated. Gemma sings 'tra la la tra la la' and sighs. The truth is one of the simpering ninnies put her little slice of cod on to the slab of ice that afternoon, and its juices became one with the ice, and now with the Panamanian economist's juices too. Gemma, wet, fishy, blushing and unsatisfied, sprays the room with Chanel No. 5.

She wears her Cardin suit for her first terrifying tutorial with three boys from Balliol College. The tutor, little black hairs on his knuckles, clenches his knees and taps a fountain pen on the mahogany desk. One of the boys presents a paper called 'Notes towards the development of a theory on the relationship between Marxism and feminism'. The tutor and the boys scribble fast little notes on the back of their folders, sometimes nodding, other times frowning, eyebrows raised. Gemma understands nothing, and when the tutor asks her to comment on the paper, bursts into tears. The men do not know what to do with this elegant glossed woman who has a reputation for scorn, strength, savoir faire, intellect, and is now squealing and squeaking like a plucked chicken behind her jasmine-yellow note pad. 'Seems like *Kapital* has been your bedtime reading these last ten years,' she weeps into her cuff. The boy who gave the talk passes her his handkerchief, shuffling his feet in irritation. He has spent long nights working on his paper and wants to discuss it; now this fat, stupid female is blubbering away all his tutorial time. Gemma cries some more

31

and runs out of the room on her pointy heels, clattering down the corridor while the boys discuss alienation.

In the corridor she bumps into Eduardo the Italian economist, who cheers her up by taking her up to his room where he whips up a steamy dish of pasta with clam sauce. While he cooks he tells her he hopes Oxford won't be swamped by 'aliens' like the red-brick universities. They snuggle up together and Gemma falls asleep, waking up with pain that surprises her. She stares at Eduardo and wills him to take it away.

Dear Gemma,

Thank you for the invitation to the ball. I have a lovely dress with scarlet netting at the bottom like a mermaid's tail. If my grandmother could see me in it she would demand I dive for beluga caviar. The only trouble is my arms and legs are covered in flea bites. Yesterday, I shampooed Krupskaya, my cat, and hope that has put an end to the central committee that debate in her fur. Is it possible for you to meet me at the station? Perhaps we can go for a drink first, I will buy you a pint of water and we can talk.

Love Lapinski.

Dearest Lapinski,

It is not a good idea to come up for the ball after all. I have promised Eduardo (my Italian economist) that I'll spend the weekend with him, and the thought of you two meeting is not calculated to send warm feelings down my spine. Perhaps you could delay the trip until I find an ideologically correct young man. Eduardo's consciousness is somewhat intractable and I have no hope of bringing him into the bright light of socialist truth. Oh well. So long as we keeeeeeep kisssssssing we don't have to talk much.

Love love love to you sugar plum
Gemma xxxxxxxx
(from a putative member of the ruling class)

In the library which she loves and where she consumes packets of rice crackers, she follows up footnote clues and obscure details on the sociology of political parties.
She thinks about Eduardo.
He is cold, cold and *dead* inside.
This thought, to her surprise, is very sexy.

'EEEEEEEeeeeeeeeeeeeeeee eeeeeeeee ee e eee eeeeeeeeeeeeee!' Gemma's orgasms are the loudest in hall. The simpering ninnies next door have to put pillows over their head or run to the bathroom or into each other's rooms. They do not always know whether she is screaming with pleasure or pain. She sounds like a squealing pig and this turns Eduardo on. While he fucks her he tells stories about killing deer on his uncle's farm, other women he has fucked, the professor he thinks is a communist; he bites her nipples and thighs, leaves blue crescent moons all over her white body. Their bed is littered with condoms, chocolate, hair, peanuts, stockings, his leather belt, knickers, cartons of milk, pitta bread, taramasalata, come stains. Gemma discovers she is brilliant at economics, better than Eduardo (he finds all sorts of ways to punish her for this), and has no problem demonstrating the difference between Returns to Scale and 'EEEEEEEEEEEEEEEEEE EEEEEEEEEEEEEEEEEEEEEEEEEEEEEEEEEEEEEEE eeeeee' Diminishing Returns to One Factor.

While my children play in the park, I am paid by men to let them put a part of their body into a part of my body. What they don't know is they are fucking a ghost. They are fucking a ghost because my spirit and soul are somewhere else but they don't care because my spirit and soul are not the most expensive parts of me. Most of my customers are businessmen with wives in the counties and shires; they spill a day's worth of wheeling and dealing into me and I receive it like sewage dumped at the bottom of the sea. Some want to beat me, some want me to pretend to love them or to pretend to be someone I am not. But that's OK, most people spend the whole of their lives pretending to be someone they are not. My names are Tremor, Gina, Ninette, Sam, Tina, Cleopatra, Iris, Suzie, Malibu, Alex, Blondie, Maggie and Stardust.

One customer wanted me to pretend to be his wife in real life – he was part of something called a REGENERATION CONSORTIUM and his firm had an open day 'party' where the local people could meet the developers in the flesh – something I do not recommend. He bought me a chiffon dress with a daisy print on it and white gloves – and I took the kids, which made him bite his lip with that sharp tooth of his. The whole event smelt of melted cheese. They'd hired eight out of work actors who went around banging people on the head with foam rubber hammers and then gave out funny hats with red, white and blue stripes on them – they looked like whip marks on pale English skin. Then the magicians started to take fake rabbits out of hats while a bored jazz band played 'Summertime' in the corner. A woman with a broken Chinese umbrella was the only one dancing, twisting her wrists to some music inside herself, while the waiters went around with sausage rolls and bowls of orange jelly on silver trays and this bloke whose wife I was shook the local community by the hand, saying, 'You're in an enterprise zone now,' to which the woman dancing replied, 'I've got my spoon stuck in the jelly.'

The highlight of the event was the free bus-tour around the area they were developing. We all trooped on to the coach and our guide was a woman in a navy blue suit called Belinda. She talked through a microphone in a robotic voice, telling us what we were passing, 'This is a waterfront conversion,' then she'd look at her clipboard and lose her place and not know where we were. The driver was ignoring her anyway (I think he'd got stoned to survive the day), so she would say, 'In the 1920s produce used to be freighted here all the way from Yorkshire,' and where she said you were, you were not – she'd point at the waterfront and it would be the railway station. Or she would say, 'On the left you will see um, what will you see, you will see something but it's not clear yet what it is that will be there for you to see.' The driver would be cruising down some high street where the police were patrolling estate agents' shop fronts because of stones being thrown at the windows, and she would tell you it was a multi-storey hotel when everyone could see it was the high street. We lost all sense of time and place and the old lady sitting behind me said she'd need a guide book to find her way home, all the while my husband muttering, 'We're restoring the city and giving it back to you.' At the end of the day he kissed me on the cheek and said loudly, 'Hope you had a pleasant day out dear — thought it would do you good to see for yourself why I am away from home so often,' and told me he was just off for a jog on the new track they had built where the share index flashes up on a screen as you run. 'We all have so much to look forward to,' he said to the woman with the Chinese umbrella who was busy stuffing six sausage rolls into her handbag. 'Pardon?' she asked politely. 'We all have so much to look forward to' he repeated. 'Yes,' she said, 'I think it goes like this but I've forgotten most of the words.

> *'sa ra bo ra*
> *ra bo ra sa*
> *sa bo bo sasa'*

My most recent customer brought his terrier dog with him — it whimpered under the bed for the ten minutes it took. He has a tattoo on his upper arm, an anchor with roses, and underneath, the word MOTHER. A lot of men have tattoos with MOTHER written on parts of their body. After he had finished he said, 'I can taste coal in my mouth' and then he confessed that something had gone wrong between him and his mother. 'It's civil war, Tremor, it's civil war between me and her,' which might be why he likes to have sex in his car to the sound of war guns – it's a game he likes to relax to.

My own son has discovered he is good at making things grow. He's got green green fingers and he's hit on the idea of growing roses in the window-box to sell at the tube station. Despite the lead from the traffic they are blooming blooming blooming. We bought everything together, the soil and seeds, read how to plant them, the light and position and how much water; I watch his seven-year-old body bent over them every morning and hope he will never have to fight a war, certainly not a civil war. I hope he will never want to beat a woman because something went wrong between me and him and he wants to take it out on her. Yesterday, when we were having supper together, my youngest daughter started to sing

> *'Lavender's blue, dilly dilly*
> *Lavender's green*
> *When I be king*
> *You shall be queen'*

and we all joined in because we know the song has a special meaning for her. She had two budgies, one called Lavender Blue and the other Lavender Green and they died seven months ago. She told me she'd buried them in the park. But yesterday she said, 'Mum, you know how I buried Lavender Blue and Lavender Green that day . . .' and I said, 'Yeah,' and she said, 'Well I didn't.' She stood up, perfectly serious, took her pencil box – one of those wooden ones with a sliding top – off the sideboard and, in front of us all, opened it up. There was Lavender Blue. Just lying there like he's having a blissful night's sleep, except his eyes have rotted. She said, 'I put your scent on him.' I said to her, 'Where's Lavender Green then?' She shook her head and said she couldn't remember where she had put him. Her brother and sister began to sing

> 'Call up your men, dilly dilly
> Set them to work
> Some shall make velvet
> And some shall make shirts'

giggling and nudging her until she gave up and told us to be quiet while she led the way to my bedroom, smiling at me to see if I was cross. She crawled under my bed, her little feet sticking out, and reached for an old shoe. Nestled in there, wrapped in tissue, was Lavender Green. She said, 'I put your scent on him too.'

So this little corpse has been lying on its back, scented, under my customers for seven months now. Just like me. I would hate my daughters to know anything about how I put a roof over their heads. My daughter has grieved in her own way for the birds she loved and lost. I don't know where I have buried all I have loved and lost but it's not in an enterprise zone. Why did they pay actors to hit us over the head with foam rubber hammers? Was it to show us they were only pretending?

Tonight, Jupiter, the god of animal metamorphoses, rules the stinking animal pits in the zoo. Urine and shit trickle into a ring of rage, a ring of starless moonless night.

The rage of animals imprisoned by a clumsy culture.

The smell of garlic oozes into the air, wafts over from the gorilla cages; the sweat of images behind the eyes, under the skin and in the cracks of lips. In the reptile house a python feeds on twelve dead rats. A mongoose eats a scorpion without removing its sting. The elephants lift up their trunks and bellow out, over London, and the refuse trucks collect the shedded skin of the day gone by to take to incinerators and burn.

Freddie lies on his belly outside the llama cage. He is covered in mud and worms, and the llama, all soft curves and very golden, bids him to speak. 'Where are your words?'

'I am unemployed,' says Freddie. 'That is to say I have no place in the scheme of things. No role to put on in the mornings and take off in the evenings. I am of the hungry species and I am alone. A stranger in a familiar land. I have no place to put my head, no thighs even in which to bury my head, no shoulder or lap or concept or cup of happiness or red rose in which to bury my head. No employment of any kind.'

'Unemployed?' says the llama. 'Oh come on. There are zillions of jobs for a slut. Why not acccccelerate, put your foot down on that steely pedal, how about a career in the citeeee? Penetrate the city like a hungry blue worm, find the worm in your self and become it. Innovation breeds success and success breeds delicious hungers of all kinds. How you do enjoy your pain, Freddie!

'Go into international finance, become a dynamic sales manufacturer in a high-growth computer company, become a senior sales consultant, a marketing manager, a business analyst for a billion-dollar corporation, become a technical support analyst with BUPA membership and relocation expenses, relocate your ambitions, relocate yourself from here to there and beyond. Relocate your head and you will find a zillion homes for it.'

'But . . .' and Freddie weeps, 'I don't know *how* to become those things. I don't know what will become of me at all. I am lost, llama, lost and lost and lost. How do I begin to become a corpuscle in a corporation?'

'OH SLUTTY SON be result-motivated! Think of those mortgage subsidies and executive benefits. Be a self-starter, be profit-motivated. Learn to Be. You need enthusiasm, no one invests in depression. Try harder and you will get the right package because you are the right person. But first you might emigrate. Pack up your head and heart and will and move to a different landscape. It is called let these words shimmer above your poor ruined head . . . The Real World.' The llama giggles.

'Oh . . . llama . . . I defend The Naked Truth of Dreams.'

'The Naked Truth of Dreams? Oh Freddie. You are indeed a funny little thing. A funny little flower.'

Freddie buries his toes in the mud and watches two apes groom each other. The giant panda stares out into nothing, melancholy as she chews a strip of sugar cane; mosquitoes wail above her head.

'What dreams are you talking about, poor Freddie?' llama's eyes widen.

'I used to have dreams, llama. But I've lost them. I search in gardens for them. It would seem it is a family I want. Do you know male seahorses give birth? They have labour pains, curl their tails around a plant stem, bend backwards and forwards with the pain, with severe cramps, until they empty their pouches. I have severe cramps and no baby. I want a baby.'

'You digress,' says llama, digging the earth with her hooves. Digging the British soil up. 'We are talking of Enterprise. Why not have a baby syndicate? If you want a family there are

> *hardware families*
> *and software families.'*

'What is there left for me to become if not a father? I will take my children to swing in parks, to swimming pools, rock them to sleep, mash them bananas . . .'

'Freddie, I fear you are talking about a Family in the bigger sense of the word. You are perhaps talking of sisterhood? Brotherhood?' Llama sticks out her tongue to catch an invisible fly.

Freddie's tears fall like pebbles on to the mud. 'I don't know what I want, llama. I would like to be happy.'

43

'Poor Freddie. You have lost your way. Lost your silky slutty senses. I confess I am rather fond of people who have lost their way.'

'Aw, fuck off, llama,' weeps Freddie. 'I just want to be loved.'

Llama scratches her ear.

'You want to be loved? Ah. Aaaaaaaaaah. But can you love, Freddie? Remember the woman with the lilies, how she sang for you, how you became a flower in her bouquet, and how you ruined her? Not because she was stupid but because she was brave. I see her now with your daughter, her little love child. It is she who fries her potatoes, pushes her on swings, buys her crayons and paper and plasticine. Your daughter makes green and blue daddies in front of the television. And the woman with the violin who mothered your son, bought him plimsolls, introduced him to The Story, took him to libraries and cinemas, played tunes for him on her fiddle to send him to sleep. And where were you, Freddie? Here with me searching for your head? Wanting children you already have? Excuse me, Freddie, I have a stone in my paw.

'If you cannot love, Freddie, do something radical with your condition, service systems that manufacture sorrow instead. In this way you will hate well rather than love badly.'

A baby chimpanzee pulls at the long black nipples of its mother, who has her arm crooked to hold its head; her mouth opens and closes in time with the suckling.

'Llama,' whispers Freddie, 'I have tried to change. I know indeed that human nature is an invented thing. I have tried to reinvent myself but confess I am reluctant to give up the little power I have on this earth. Yes, I am weeping again, I don't know when I'll ever stop or why. It seems there is no longer any grass to dream on. I hurt, llama, and I want someone to make me better. Have I really missed out on my children? I try to dream about women who have loved me but they refuse to appear. I want peace of mind. I want some peace but I don't know what it is. Anything to get rid of this . . . stuff . . . inside me, this fear, these tears, this shaking. I would shoot guns and thrust bayonets through flesh to distract me from myself; I would whip, torture, wrestle, drive racing-cars over cliffs to distract me from myself; jump from helicopters, throw hand grenades to distract me from myself; I would march right left right screaming orders in my throat, obeying orders in my throat, to distract me from myself. I would build muscles I never knew I had, to distract me from myself.'

Llama shuts her honey eyes. Her belly rises and falls. It is as if her breath is a gentle wind; it makes the salt on Freddie's cheeks smart and sting. He notices three cards pinned to her cage. The blue card says History, the white card says Behaviour and the pink card says Medical Record.

10.15 Specimen sounds as if she is coughing slightly.

10.40 Specimen vomited a little fluid.

1.10 Specimen restless.

1.40 Specimen has stomach contractions.

2.00 Specimen lying on back with periodic grunts.

2.30 No change in position.

4.10 Specimen throwing her weight against cage bars.
Seems agitated.

5.10 Specimen shows evidence of some nasal discharge.

5.30 Specimen shows no reaction to noise.

5.45   Specimen refusing food. Eyes shut.
6.00   Specimen runs and falls over on occasions.
7.00   Specimen co-ordination much improved.
        Saliva around mouth.
If no change tomorrow take swab.

'Are you ill, llama?' whispers Freddie
'Are you ill, Freddie?' whispers llama.
'I think I might be very sick, yes, llama. And I cannot afford health.'

Llama smiles patronizingly. 'The only freedom you have, Freddie, is the freedom to want more sugar. I am no barbarian. I do not come from your country. By a strange set of circumstances I find myself locked up here. How strange it is I find myself teaching you the hieroglyphics of your culture.'

'Oh God,' Freddie howls. 'Oh God.' He scoops up mud and begins to eat it. 'Llama . . . perhaps . . . you could . . . could just bite my artery here. Put me out of my misery.'

'My teeth are blunt,' says llama. 'The zoo keeper filed them down.'

Freddie lies on his back and listens to the owls hoot into the night.

The lion shuts his eyes. He dreams he is lying in the shade of the acacia trees. The sound of that strange piano from an invisible part of the city dips in and out of the pictures behind his eyes. To the lion it is the wind. In his dream he prowls over to a nearby waterhole only to find it on fire. Fire over water. The smell of burning flesh wafts over the long bleached grasses. He opens his eyes. The grass has turned to cement.

*

Outside the zoo, a young boy and girl in their early twenties sit against a wall. A tattoo on their upper arms says THE INNO-CENTS. Their eyes are closed as they sing in harmony

'And then the knave begins to snarl
And the hypocrite to howl;
And all his good friends show their private ends
And the eagle is known from the owl'

They both think about hitching to a forest where they spent two summers and remember one particular tree. A pine tree. But the forests have been blown down in a small hurricane, the night the Stock Exchange crashed, and no one is planting things any more. They remember the evergreen of this tree and how it collected water on the tips of its needles; they would take it in turns to rip off their clothes and one of them stand under the tree while the other shook it by the trunk as it bowed this way and that way and little drops of water sprinkled the head of whoever stood under it.

The Innocents open their eyes. They feel the wall behind their backs and take deep breaths of the city's air.

Dear Lapinski,

It is so HOT here in New York. I'm sitting naked at the table writing this. Sweat keeps dripping on to the page. Eduardo and I are now married. He works in Rome and flies over to see me at weekends. Instead of diamonds he brings me sachets of sugar and salad cream from the aeroplane – I have a whole closet full of them.

As words have never been our strong point we sit in front of the television flicking the remote control and eating our way through cartons of popcorn. The wedding was wonderful. When I cut the cake I cut my finger too and blood dripped all over the icing the Italian baker had taken three months to make into the columns of the opera-house. It was OK. Eduardo has always found blood sexy and sucked my finger for the photographer. My lips are covered in blisters. It always happens before I have an appraisal of my performance by the company. This is difficult to write. I feel very far away from you, both in experience and distance. Last time we met you looked at me as if all the worst predictions you made for me at

*fifteen had come true. More sweat. Blanche would have worn a
floral wrapper but otherwise it's very Tennessee Williams.*

Love Gemma

Gemma has become The Banker; a super-rich money market-
eer whose qualities of commercial acumen, aggression, energy,
contact ability (most of her colleagues at Oxford), motivation,
ego drive and adaptability earn her a salary she will not disclose.
She has closed up like a seaflower, her voice on the phone is
expressionless and brief; at the hairdresser, under the bright lights,
she catches up on sleep. Nights alone are very still and black, she
prefers to sleep with people around her. She pays a special consultant to buy and choose furniture for her New York apartment,
a mixture of old and new: a telephone from a 1930s Hollywood
movie, two chaise-longues from an auction, a Perspex table, a
bunch of glass poppies that light up at night, two Magrittes for the
white walls, theatre posters from sell-out Broadway musicals, a
sculpture made from nails. Her wardrobe is full of navy suits
and leather pumps to match, she long ago threw out the Mexican smocks, orchids, glittering shoes of her school days and
camouflaged herself in the discreet colour and cloth of a feminized male uniform. Her towelling robe is yellow and so is the
bathroom soap; such attention to detail is what the consultant is
paid for.

She jokes that she is not complimented on her bone structure
any more, but on her bonus structure. Yesterday the blisters on
her lips popped. On summer evenings, The Banker sits on her

tiny balcony chewing Swiss chocolate and aspirins, watching the Empire State Building twinkle in the distance.

From dawn to dusk she is surrounded by computer screens and telephones. The day starts with a pep talk from the company analyst and then she begins selling. In her lunch hour she either has a pregnancy test (she does not want to be pregnant) or eats bagels on the edge of the desk watching the screens. Instant reactions to information is her skill. The slightest flicker and her jaws stop chewing on turkey mayonnaise. Her ruby nails dig into the black silk of her stockinged thighs, every rip equals a decision, and she has to buy them in bulk each week. Torn, laddered, full of tiny holes, they are her calendar to judge the stress of each day.

On Saturday mornings she works out in the bank's gymnasium and then meets a colleague for a Mexican meal. She has got short of breath but her lips still shine. Sometimes when Eduardo is asleep by her side she sobs like a wolf cub. The strange thing is there are no tears, she is dry-eyed even after hours of sobbing. Once when Eduardo woke up to find her body shaking and heaving he put his arms around her and asked what was wrong. She just buried her head under the pillow, lying on her stomach, and continued to sob, sometimes surfacing to look at the clock.

Eduardo thinks about the week ahead and the small sleek whores in Bangkok, always smiling and ready to please. They know grief is not good for business.

In the morning he takes her shopping. He buys her spiky shoes, suspenders, petticoats, wigs she will never wear, a briefcase with a combination lock and a small revolver. She buys him the best cigarettes, starched white shirts, a cap with checks the shop assistant said was his tartan and twelve pairs of socks. Afterwards they eat ice-cream in parlours all over the city and then she takes him to the Waldorf where there is a little red bus in the window with HOVIS AND BUTTER FOR TEA written across its side. 'Makes me think of home,' she tells him as the Barts Bells chime twelve. Her sobbing fits stop and she knows they will never, never happen again. She is shaking hands with a fat man in grey flannels and a bow tie who thanks her for her help and promotes her to their branch in London. He says, 'You are a star, climb to the top and don't look down.' She says, 'I guess I'll miss the pace here Joe,' and jumps into the scarlet company car. As she looks in the mirror we catch each other's eye. We are startled voyeurs. The last time we were this close was when she took the glass of hot chocolate from my hand and put it to her lips.

Her eye is as blue as meat,
  We stare into each other and then she cuts me out.
  She shuts her eye.

The Banker taps her silicone fingernail on the window of her Cadillac. It is as if she wants to tap the irritation out of her self. She turns up the air conditioning, stops at the traffic lights, brushes her hair, glosses her lips, swallows vitamins, eats chocolate, checks her watch. The back seat is piled high with Gucci bags. As she boards the aeroplane to Heathrow, gold wedding ring glistening in the sun, she turns to me and says in transatlantic English, 'Don't pride your self on being a small bird perched on my shoulder, Lapinski. I am just about to enter a huge bird, to be carried through the clouds and home again. You are a still-born bird somewhere at the back of my head, a cold-war baby who wants to make peace when there is no peace to be had. Life *is* a nightmare, it's more interesting like that. You are no great shakes. It's my job to invent reality, not fiction. I invent the world. You just figure out ways of surviving in it. You are the dispossessed cringing somewhere on the corner of this earth. I am in its centre, a bright burning light, and you in the corner will be dazzled.'

The air hostess offers her mineral water and prawn mousse. Down below, people get smaller and smaller as the engines roar and The Banker melts little dabs of orange shellfish on her tongue.

While the hares at John F. Kennedy Airport race the plane on the runway, an old man in Piccadilly, London, screams in the middle of the road, hands stretched above his silver hair. A line of cars comes to a standstill; the people in them are secretly afraid to get out and move him on. They laugh nervously behind the wheel; his screams pulse through their hearts. The Innocents watch him. They know his name is Mac and that he is homeless too. When he has finished screaming they saunter into the road and help him to the pavement. Mac says, 'Okay you bandits give the old shaman a smoke. See this white skin over my left eye? I'm screaming so as to break it . . . to get to the green underneath.'

On the edge of the motorway, a woman who wears earrings made from seashells sits on a high stool by the stainless steel meatbelt. She remembers a dream in which great clumps of small eggs, like spawn, leak from her and are put on a slide in a laboratory.

Deborah Levy

Her mother, sister and a nurse are present. The nurse tells her that the red eggs are normal, but there is a chance that the white eggs contain 'abnormalities.' The name on her medical file is Saint Martha.

An aeroplane has just flown over. It even drowned the sound of the machines on the meatbelt, which is quite something because they hum within as well as outside me; we have become one body. I am doing the night shift and miss my friend The Poet who calls me Saint Martha (she says it's a promotion) – she not been to work for three days now. I don't know where she is but I suspect she is trying to do something impossible. The lights from the factory guide planes that fly over us. The Alsatians outside bark at them. Sometimes I wish they'd just crash into us and we'd all die very quickly in a pool of duty-free gin. When for that one moment I could no longer hear the sound of the machines I thought I had died, that my heart had stopped and I had become meat too, splattered over the walls and floor.

I ached to be different from the women in my home town. But it's hard to be enchanting and carefree and spiritual when you're dead broke. I wanted either to take part in the world, to taste it, to dare search out joy and claim it, or not be here at all. I wanted there to be more to life than just surviving it. I wanted and I wanted. When I went to university, someone said, 'Are you going to piss in the outside loo in silk knickers then?'

I laughed when I was a student and first fell in love because I realized to be in love is to dream the other person instead of seeing them as they actually are –he was thrilling because he was a big bad boy from Barcelona and wore blood-red espadrilles even in the English rain. Some afternoons we would skip lectures and climb up on to the roof garden a friend had lent us with a bottle of wine, and fuck for hours; we talked about books, our lips wet with Rioja and each other. He said, 'In Spain every man is the toreador/Christ: we like to conquer death and pierce our flesh.' If I was brought up on chips and the Easter fair, he was brought up on paella and Mass. We made no plans for the future – we assumed our lives would be rich in ideas and events, that we would always be curious, searching, full of questions and sensa-tions. We assumed this because we made each other feel beautiful and interesting; I never thought it possible, then, that ideas could be bashed into stupid blue meat, and people encouraged to eat them like fast-food burgers. I often wonder where he is now, what he is doing, and whether he still feels able to conquer death.

When I visit my home town it's like going back to the scene of some silent, unrecorded massacre. Newspapers full of obsolete tragedies flap around the gasworks like dying birds. Condoms cringe in gutters. Pregnant prostitutes stand on street corners. There are regular floods of cancers for the undertaker to get rich on; cancer is gold to him. Young unemployed men and women suicide themselves all the time; leave ragged notes hidden in secret places for someone who might have cared for them to find, testimonies to their punctured spirit and shame and sorrow. If all their testimonies were put together they would make a new Bible, its prophets dead in battered cars, garages, and the bottoms of cliffs. There is a war on. Everyone is separated and afraid. It is as if we have been robbed of a language to describe the bewildered brokenness we inhabit. Best to leave and learn another language.

Last year I took my first ever holiday in Europe. I did not find myself in some golden paradise – but on an industrial beach, blue and pink corrugated iron shacks on the shore. Little fires and local people frying sardines. Dogs asleep on the sand. Football posts. Gulls with filthy wings swooping down for sewage and bread. High-rise flats. Patches of grass. A goat. The sad thing is I felt perfectly at home. I bought some candles from a holy shop with handmade roses climbing down the sides. A woman was begging as if her hand was made that way. On the last day, I took a bus to the nearest big city. Ate pork and cockles in cafés that smelt of drains. Drank lots of little cups of coffee with sweet almond cake, smoked strange cigarettes in red packets. Next to the big international shops, traders had set up barrows heaped with nuts, cheap glass, earrings made from shells (I'm wearing them now) and flowers, so many flowers, sold by gypsies from the country. Organ grinders, church bells, chestnut sellers, chocolates filled with liqueurs distilled in Gothic monasteries, taxis, trams, piazzas, boulevards, tables and chairs out on the pavements in the sun and tourists taking photographs of everything. Men kissing each other, twice on the cheek, holding each other as they talked. Mothers and daughters with blossom in their buttonholes. They reminded me of a woman at home, with blue lips because she had a bad heart, who pinned a flower from her garden on to my heart. Once I went to a café with a huge clock on the wall; its hands kept swinging out of time with real time, so the waiters had to climb up the ladder to put it right. I went to art galleries full of the work of modernists and I went to bookshops to look for native poets in translation. My hair started to curl when it had always been straight. I read newspapers in the marble foyers of grand hotels and when I got bored, slipped into churches to see the frescos, listen to the service, watch people cross themselves in a trance. Among the elaborate gold leaf on the walls, one painting shocked – a priest standing against a cold snow sky and, stretched across the sky, a thin icy spiked line of barbed wire, the expression in his eyes chilled, as if at the moment the artist caught him he had lost his faith and was filled with unspeakable fear. I gazed at statues, touched them, sat under them reading maps, my fingers sticky with watermelon, legs tanned. I met a scientist and she took me home to meet her family, as if she regarded me as an important person who was worth getting to know. I played with her children, drank her wine, talked for hours about where I was from – she was trying to put me together, understand what sort of world I came from, but I didn't want her to understand because then I'd have to live in the world she was trying to put together. I wanted to live somewhere else.

That aeroplane has frayed my nerves. And they are not too good at the moment. I wake up coughing and my bronchitis seems to be eternal. These days the most innocent of things can have a myriad fearful associations for me. Perhaps it was not a good idea to be promoted from Martha to Saint Martha, even though I know The Poet was joking. Did the saints feel psychically assaulted and scared, like I do? I feel there is something leaking from me, I think it is hope, that I need to save myself but I don't know how to. The lights are beginning to dim which means the night shift is nearly over. It is as if we women working on the meatbelt are returning to each other after a long separation and are startled by the distance we have travelled. Once, when I was watching The Poet work opposite me, for one mad and possibly saintly moment I thought she looked like a Messiah with no cross to hang on. The job of The Poet, like the Messiah, is essentially to prepare the imagination of the people to receive metaphors of all kinds. I have a feeling that right now she is trying to turn herself into a fish. She loves a good joke.

7.15   Swab taken from specimen.

7.30   Specimen runs and falls over on occasions.

8.30   Specimen stands and falls over on occasions.

8.40   Specimen shows evidence of distress.

The llama's breath rises and falls. Like the dollar thinks Freddie. He wants to hold her. Bury his face in her fur. He sticks his hand through the cage bars but he cannot reach her. She seems to be sleeping and shivering at the same time. An aeroplane flies over the zoo and the animals become restless. The sky is scarred with a thick white line. The chief gorilla smooths the scar on his own chest with hands that are not so different from the hands of the old zoo keeper who rolls oranges into his cage every evening. The animals call to each other, ears alert, they murmur, scratch themselves, bellow out into the thick night of the city. It is as if the passing of this winged beast is an omen for some terrible happening in the future. The bird cages are full of fallen feathers; in a corner the Marabou stork hides her head under her wing. The white-tailed mongoose eats without tasting what it is he's eating. Toads croak. The cats lick invisible wounds with long sideways sweeping movements of their tongues. The elephants plaster mud on their skin, roll about in the dust and rub themselves against the wall of their compound. Their ears flap and spread, grey circles of time imprinted on their mud-soaked flesh, just as the hearts of trees have circles of time marked within themselves. The elephants dimly remember moonlit nights drifting through the bush stripping bark; tonight time seems to have stopped and the wind is hot.

In the city, three Cabinet ministers in navy serge suits, cufflinks and well-polished brogues dump their briefcases on a hotel bed and pour themselves large gin and tonics. They raise their glasses and sing

> *'England here*
> *England there*
> *England every fucking where.'*

Outside, on the high street, people put bits of plastic into a brick wall and in return get money. They carry their personal number around with them, in their sleep, during meals, love play, in swimming baths and offices. The computer in the wall is hot, like the forehead of a person with a fever, burning into the bricks and mortar of Europe.

09.00 Specimen shows evidence of discharge from eyes.
09.30 Specimen refuses to stand up.
10.30 Specimen still shows evidence of distress.

The llama's eyes have turned into a lake. She rolls on to her belly. Freddie thinks he can see her tail flicker, as if she is diving into her self. He touches his forehead for no reason at all. She looks like a fish with fur. Her belly is silvery grey. Freddie realizes he has been looking up into the sky which seems to be a great fathomless pool of inky water, and on the rippleless surface he can see the reflection of the llama's thoughts. At this moment she is a salmon, still and silent as the beginning of the world.

A woman with green wispy hair bends and bows over the black keys of her piano like a small tender willow. It is she who plays only those notes forbidden by the Catholic Church in the days of the Inquisition, who scents herself with Chinese cedar and twenty-five oils that are not for the timid, whose ribs stick out like needles, whose music spreads itself over all bedsit London, music that is full of questions, discord and joyful contradictions. The Anorexic Anarchist.

She says, 'No no no, Lapinski . . . I will not let you be an autocrat. I will break the pattern of your summoning which I hear through my little diseased cherry tree that refuses to blossom in this time of the accountant, prison warder, soldier, in this time when our common land is used to store nuclear icons, and battery chickens become golden nuggets in boxes that destroy the air we breathe. In this time when pigs become lumps of sorrow soaked in preservatives and people register their personal decay in solitary massacres . . . yes I will break the pattern of your summoning. I will sow the seeds of chaos and disorder about your shoes, both left and right. I have a cake baking in the oven, can you smell the vanilla? Come here. Closer than that. I am going to transform *you*, but not before I have had a bath to cleanse me from all the television screens that go on at night.' Her bones crack against the white porcelain of the bath. 'I am an antibody fighting fighting fighting . . . Come closer, Lapinski, you will be Marie Antoinette.'

I am Marie Antoinette. My bouffant of white cottonwool hair is tangled with barbed wire and birds; soldiers shoot out of my curls. I am standing outside a blue bank in the high street, a great hooped dress swirling about my hips. My lips red as glacé cherries. Two men who call themselves aides stand on either side of me. They wear mirrored sunglasses and one of them looks a little like Freddie; a white worm wriggles on his shoulderpad. Who's your worm dancing for?' a woman carrying a violin asks him, and then takes a bite of her apple where she hopes no worms lurk. A huge cake stands on a silver trolley in front of me, iced with a map of the world. I have a metre ruler in my hand and as people go by I ask them if they would like a piece of cake. If they say yes, I put their portion of the world on to a banking slip one of the aides passes to me, with EAT CAKE in the little boxes where it says ACCOUNT NUMBER. The Anorexic Anarchist plays the trombone behind me, sometimes stopping to wheeze the concertina hung on leather straps around her neck, or to nibble sunflower seeds which are the only thing that keep her alive.

When the world is eaten, we take the soldiers out of my hair and bury them under a spindly sapling trying to grow in a crack in the pavement. A little boy makes a wreath out of his milkshake carton. Two lovers kiss on the grave, a small city-dance of leather and suede. I think of my father and mother and how they made love on the marble slab of a war memorial – perhaps it is the shame of the same species murdering each other so often that demands an affirmation of life, murdering each other in the heart, lung, arm, head, thigh, groin.

We are in a rowing boat. I am rowing. The Anorexic Anarchist rubs Nivea into her sparrow arms. The sun is warm and gentle. She closes her eyes, lids delicate, transparent, slivers of tiny veins. With her eyes shut she looks like a leaf. She trails her fingers in the lake. 'Contentment, Lapinski, is going to meet someone you love on a full stomach. Happiness is going to meet someone you love on an empty stomach.'

She invites me to her home. On the floor is a clay bowl and inside it her lunch – two glistening spinach leaves. Her room smells of the wax candles she burns by the dozen while playing the piano. And of bread. It is in her bread that she creates the most beautiful anarchy. She puts everything into it, beer, rice, lentils, cumin, rye, yoghurt, depending on what she wants the bread to do to whoever eats it. It is the coming together, the convergence of everything she yearns for in the world. She makes bread that is full of ingredients she is attracted to but she wants to be empty. She is trying to make the world less of something by making herself less of something as she oils her emaciated legs and arms, and she is teaching herself how to walk a tightrope. The rope is just six inches above the floor and her feet grip it as she shuffles across, arms flapping on either side. On the fifth step she stops, straightens up and points to the two spinach leaves. 'Eat your spinach, Lapinski.' She walks another step, it seems to take a hundred years. 'I have this little thing I do, Lapinski, when I put food on a fork, it can never touch my lips.' She smiles. 'I have walked the tightrope all my life. Now I'm trying to learn how to get to the other side.'

On the meatbelt blood is being spilled. Someone has been injured. The blades of the machines are still whirring. Seashells scatter across the floor. Someone's left hand is no longer attached to their wrist. The light is very bright. Women pick up the shells and put them in the pockets of their overalls. They do not know whether they are awake or asleep. Monster burgers slide down the belt, unattended as makeshift bandages are stripped from clothing and women haul themselves back from places of their own making – back to this scene, this room where the very real smell of blood is soaking into the paisley print of someone's headscarf, wrapped around the wrist of the injured woman known as Saint Martha, but mostly called Marth. The meat creates its own dimensions, patterns, becomes itself – a herd of beasts. The smell of blood mingling with perfumes dabbed on the temple and pulse points, and the ghostly fragrance of scents that have been imagined only five minutes before, the skin of a lover, the creases of a child, cardamon in a curry. Two bewildered women hold the shells to their ears – the sea sounds poisoned, slow and heavy as if she pulls towards the moon but cannot get back again. The women feel dizzy with the light, time has stopped, so much human blood trickling into the meat that was once four legs, a head, two eyes, a tail. They wander about pressing emergency buttons that do not work because they make no sound and the floor manager is out to lunch.

What a cunt. Lapinski told me I have no imagination. What do I need that for when my life could not be better than it is? On a good day, I've got quite a lot of things to look forward to. When they privatize prisons and water, I'll be there for a slice of the cake. Yesterday I went to a pleasure dome with a colleague. We had T-Bone, as a matter of fact. I could have ordered three T-Bones but my stomach won't take the stretch which pisses me off because I could have more of anything I want. Then we came back here and got rat-arsed on a bottle of Scotch. And another one. I didn't feel a hundred per cent this morning. The boss crept up to me in his famous posh boy brogues and said something like 'We don't carry any fat, you know.' Well I suppose fear is an executive tool, but fat? My mother went without so I could sleep at night without eating my fists. No one is going to make me feel bad about ordering Three T-Bones and giving two of them to my mother, but she doesn't want my money. I visited her last week-end, she was playing chess with her neighbour and when I walked in (dressed specially in a new shirt) she said, 'Son, you're a prat. Look after your queen, Mrs R.' One day I'll shoot her and it'll break my heart. I could buy her a car but she doesn't respect me enough to say yes, yes son, thank you. Dunno how she wanted her son to grow up. Dunno what she wants of me. Tonight I'm going to a charity ball to help raise money for a children's hospital – they're raffling off a helicopter. I'll get wrecked on champagne and help save babies with bone disease at the same time.

You have to take and then give a little bit back. You take a load and give back a slice. If I were to become strawberry jam under a tube train, the computers would carry on dealing without me; there are plenty more like me to feed the canon, to bribe and bully, to fill the bars and toy-town houses, to talk the talk and wear the uniform, to sell on dodgy everything and collect the annual bonus. People in my home town still talk about my father. He is a well-missed man. They don't miss me and I don't miss them.

Hopefully the firm will relocate me soon. To the South-East or around. No Lapinski there. No glue sniffers there. No Greek sausages, salt fish or funny bananas in the shops there. The flower beds have no weeds in them and no one stands out in a crowd. The publicans serve who they want to serve because they own the place and they like serving me.

A whole fresh salmon wrapped in foil with butter and herbs bakes in the oven. The napkins on the table are pale pink French linen, the cutlery silver, the glasses the thinnest, most fragile crystal. Marlene Dietrich croons from the compact disc player.

I, Lapinski, am in front of the mirror again. It seems The Banker and I are destined to meet backwards through the reflective surface of this glass. It was by the mirror my grandmother used to watch herself cry, first as a child and later as an adult. She was too proud to show her tears; instead when she felt the need to weep she would take from the drawer one of her many handkerchiefs, fold it on her lap, take off her eyeglasses and ritually begin. When she married and her husband caught her weeping one day by the glass he shook her by the shoulders so hard her hair, which she always scraped into a bun, fell loose and her combs scattered on the floor. 'Why are you so cross?' she had asked him. He replied tenderly putting the combs back in her hair, 'I often want to cry because I hoped I would marry a beautiful woman – and what did I fall in love with? A woman with a wart under her arm and a mouth like a crack in a pie. But do I cry? No. I do not cry because she is everything to me and if she is sad I want to know why.'

They opened a bottle of vodka kept for special occasions, talking about their good days and less good days and the neighbour who kept carp in the bath ; it was only when they had finished half the bottle they remembered their daughter (my mother) was skating that afternoon to an audience of hundreds of school children. They arrived drunk, dishevelled and flushed, and embarrassed my mother by cheering loudly throughout her dance; afterwards she said their breath melted the ice and made her fall.

Through the looking glass I can see The Banker. She is slipping into a charcoal silk dress, goose pimples on her arms. Eduardo is shaving in the bathroom and shouts at her for leaving water on the floor after her bath. She flosses her teeth and says the maid will clean it up in the morning. Eduardo calls her 'cats-breath' and playfully holds the razor up to her throat making slicing gestures. 'This is how you slice Parma ham,' he says, and then tells her she's lost her sense of humour.

Outside, the Innocents sit by the river drinking a bottle of sweet sherry. The girl has a violin bow in one hand and a cigarette in the other. She bows the boy's ear and he makes the noise of a violin in his throat. Fifty yards away a policeman watches over them; the boy now takes the bow and runs it over the girl's ear. She makes the noise of a violin in her throat. When they have finished the sherry they throw the bottle in the river. A helicopter hovers above them.

*

Jerry puts the last touches to his dinner table. With his golden ringlets curling under his earlobes, pale blue eyes and dimples he looks like a baby angel. At twenty-nine he has developed a slight lisp and when he smiles his tongue sticks out between his Cupid lips. A pianist/composer, quite famous in particular circles, his forte is to enchant his audience and introduce them to art and culture. He gives concerts for minor aristocrats in their rural homes, also at stately houses rented for the evening by various corporations and at numerous glitzy dinner parties. His experimental lisp and genuine love of shortbread baked by his adoring grandmother, who he lives with and who is also getting dressed for supper, all make him a delicious slightly wayward treat. He is much sought after and well-fucked by the sons of lords and dukes before they marry the women they will breed with and despise.

At this moment Grannie Bird, as she is called, is clipping a pair of ancient jet earrings on to her ears. She powders her soft smooth cheeks and remembers that she left her pot of rouge in the box at the Opera House in Milan.

The boy and girl watch the bottle of sherry bob up and down on the water. After a while the girl takes out a little box and shows it to the boy. Inside the box is a perfect set of long white false fingernails. She begins to put them on and the boy pushes back her cuticles with his own bitten fingernails. The policeman is baffled.

Eduardo, The Banker, Jerry and Grannie Bird sit at the candle-lit table drinking a light white wine with their fennel and Parmesan salad. Marlene sings 'Fallink in love again' and Eduardo, who has

73

taken off his shoes, searches for his wife's thighs under the table. Jerry is telling everyone about his last concert and how the host has promised to take him skiing in Europe for a weekend. Grannie Bird smiles; her teeth are like porcelain, and her blue eyes small and bright. 'You will look like a little angel flying over the snow. Be sure to keep your fingers warm.' The smell of salmon cooking wafts through the kitchen. Suddenly she says, 'My dear, you smell of roses.' She moves nearer The Banker and breathes deeply. 'Roses and roses and roses.' She gazes up into the chandelier. The Banker tells her there must be rose in her perfume. 'Ah that is what it must be,' sighs Grannie Bird, putting her knife and fork together. Eduardo tells them he has commissioned an artist to make prints of Warhol into tiles for their bathroom. The Banker tells Jerry she lost a hundred thousand pounds in the computer that morning and how it took her an hour to find it again. Eduardo nudges his toe under her knicker elastic. Jerry wraps one of his ringlets round and round his plump finger. Marlene sings 'I can't help it'; Grannie Bird wipes each corner of her lips with a napkin. Suddenly she moves back her chair and begins to tell a story.

'On the tube this morning three Irish children, they must have been five, seven and nine years old, got into my carriage, and in their hands, my dear,' she smiles at The Banker, 'were the most beautiful pink and red roses. Long-stemmed and alert as a rose should be, they smelt like you, Gemma, it is your fragrance that reminds me. And these children started begging from passengers. First the little girl came up to me, held the rose under my nose and said, "Give us some money for food then." I shook my head and she went away. Then the little boy came up to me, his eyes as green as green, his hair shaved off, face heart-shaped and . . .' Grannie Bird puts her fingertips together '. . . tragic. He also pinned the rose right under my nose and said, "Give us some money for food then." I shook my head. He said, "Please please please please please please please," pushing the rose into my face until I found myself blushing and delved into my pocket for some loose change. He said, "Give us a pound, I don't want less than a pound." I gave him substantially less than a pound, just the few coins I had. Perhaps twenty pence. All the time he pressed the rose into my face. "Please please please please I grew these flowers with Mama." '

Grannie Bird makes the sound of a little dog whining please please please. Jerry giggles and makes a rose from his pink napkin, which he presents to her with a little bow of his golden head.

'Thank you, Sir.'

She smiles at Eduardo.

'That rose smelt like the roses of my childhood. Of the world I grew up in. The woods a haze of bluebells, oh they looked like a Monet, and the light . . . if you appreciate light . . . early-morning mists, cuckoos in spring, the woodpecker, pheasants, wild rabbits. That rose made me think of my own mother in her gardening gloves, pruning her rose bushes; she planned her roses every year and people who visited from the city always took one or two back with them. English roses. When they were full-blown, petals would fall on the walnut sideboard, there were vases of them all over the house, and I would save them to press in heavy old books.'

Eduardo shuts his eyes. He is bored. His toe wriggles from side

75

to side, Gemma silently mouths 'EEEEEEK'; Marlene sings 'Vhat am I to do?' and Jerry fills everyone's glass.

'My world was a peaceful thoughtful world. We basked in gardens we ourselves had created. Gentle sunlight, straw hats, white gloves, scones, homemade jams, lazy days picking blackberries in September, happy happy days. We knew the names of the children of all our servants and never forgot their birthdays. Bees hovered about the lavender bushes, our cook gave us muslin from the kitchen to make sachets of the stuff for our top drawers. My parents honeymooned in Europe for two years in a horse-drawn caravan. The house was always full of artists and actors. I spent my childhood on horses and my adolescence posing under the apple tree for young men in silk scarves. My father was a wonderful host and my mother, although she never made much fuss about it, painted little watercolours, with brushes especially imported from China. Dragonflies we thought of as fairies, yes those were happy day. My uncle tickling trout, rugs and hampers and lemonade. A hundred strokes to the hair last thing at night. We appreciated life. Lived it to the full, wanted it to last for ever and ever. Do you know, my dears, I have seven generations of earls in my larynx . . .'

Jerry nudges her arm. 'Grannie, tell us about the little boy.'

'Oh yes. I gave him the money and he went away. I shouted "GIVE ME THE ROSE THEN" . . . he looked as if he was going to kill me. You see, although other passengers had given money, they had not asked for the rose. They were just glad to be left alone. I am made of sterner stuff, and shouted again, "I gave you the money now you can give me the rose." So he gave it to me.

76

And then he started to cry. His sister rummaged in her pockets and found a pencil which she gave to him and he went round with that instead, holding it under people's noses as if it was a rose. And when someone gave him money and demanded the pencil his sister gave him her hair slide . . . she just took it out of her hair there and then . . . he went around with that saying, "Give us some money for food then?" And when someone took the hair slide his younger sister turned out her pockets and found a half-eaten sandwich. So he put that under some gent's nose and the man said, "You've got food," pointing to the sandwich. "What do you want money for?"

The Banker claps her hands. 'Play for us, Jerry.' Eduardo joins in, 'Play play play play.' Grannie Bird leaves the table, her long black velvet dress whispering along the carpet as she walks to the kitchen and opens the oven. The candles flicker as Jerry sings

> *'Oh, Susannah won't you answer*
> *with her hand her face she's hiding*
> *some adventure, some adventure I shall see.'*

Eduardo is telling his wife about his meeting with a Japanese financier at an oyster and champagne bar in Soho. How they both agreed when the deal had been made that business was not too difficult and totally immoral which is why they both liked it. Jerry tosses his ringlets

> *'With her hand her face is hiding.'*

Grannie Bird carries in the salmon. It is so big it flops over the sides of the baking tray. She puts it down on the table. It is steaming. She unwraps the foil and is just about to poke a long thin knife into its belly, when the salmon seems to take its last breath. It rises from the dish and gasps. Melted butter runs over its eyes. The Banker, who has been embarrassed by fish before, looks at it with interest. She bites her lip. Grannie Bird says to Jerry, 'Cut the fish will you darling.' Jerry takes the knife from her, his little plump hands shaking slightly. Eduardo moves his toe inside his wife's knickers. The Banker says, 'Eeeeeeek.' Grannie Bird fiddles with the cutlery. Jerry cuts into the fish and Eduardo's plate is held out for the first sliver of pale orange pink flesh.

The terrible strange sight of ten minutes ago is uncommented on, as if saying something will confirm it actually happened. No one touches their salmon. They eat the petits pois, potatoes, broccoli, break bread rolls and dip them into the mayonnaise and parsley sauce, pushing the fish to the side of their plates, talking of summer holidays, the exchange rate, property, obituary columns, and magazines they subscribe to.

Grannie Bird puts a bottle of port, five jade glasses and a whole Stilton on the table. She tells them the way to eat it is to scoop out the middle with a little silver spoon. Jerry hands round a bowl of walnuts, singing

> *'This is shameless*
> *what presumption!*
> *I forbid you to come near.'*

Grannie Bird pops chocolates on her grandson's tongue and peals with laughter as he pretends to pant for more. Eduardo puts his shoes back on and sits on the cream leather settee with a glass of port. A block of passion-fruit sorbet melts unnoticed on the trolley. The Banker looks at the salmon. She is curious and takes a flat silver knife to cut a tiny piece of flesh off its belly, puts it on her tongue and chews it very slowly as if assessing its flavour. I catch her eye as she spits it out into her napkin and re-glosses her lips. She gargles with rosé and spits that out into the napkin too. As she breaks a match in half and picks her teeth with it, she turns to me, cheeks flushed.

'I think, Lapinski, this is the terrible trick of one of your friends. This fish has the possessed eye of a poet and tastes just as useless. In fact it tastes like a melancholy misfit. I have always hated poetry, I prefer hard mathematics or even hard drugs. Do you really think that in consuming this *pescado* I would consume its ideas? I have spat them out again and again. And what is The Idea? That there are thirteen ways of looking at a blackbird? Give it to me, I'll take it to the market and show you sixty ways of looking at it. Poets are fuckwits. They try and legislate with language but they don't have the roubles to bribe. On my aunt's salmon farm they stroke the belly of hen salmon to squeeze out their eggs for breeding. Well, I have squeezed you out too.'

This is shameless
what presumption
I forbid you to come near.

Jerry sticks his tongue into the middle of the Stilton, eases it in a little further and looks at Eduardo.

'Do you think I am a cannibal, Lapinski? That I eat consciousness? You fucking piss-artist. That you should try and infiltrate me so deviously. You have delusions of grandeur.'

> *so coy then*
> *just to tease me . . . la la la*
> *I know why you're waitin' here*

Jerry's tongue is covered in Stilton. Eduardo has fallen asleep.

'You fucking village idiot. You've spent too long in steamy kitchens making dumplings and *kasha* for broken people in broken shoes.'

She looks for her car keys.

> *I do like to be beside the seaside*
> *I do like to be beside the sea*

Grannie Bird sings in a quivering high voice, swaying her velvet hips in time with the piano.

The Banker slams her foot down on the accelerator of her Mercedes; smoke steams out of the exhaust and her hands, on the wheel, are white with fury. It is as if years of anger and fatigue are burning through her charcoal silk body. This time when she looks into the mirror she does not cut me out. Her eye is blue as petrol.

'You, Lapinski, are the dinosaur trapped in ice from the age of slow-moving beings. I sit on trains rolling through the remains of the Industrial Revolution in a first class carriage reserved for me, briefcase by my side, computer on my lap, telephone under my chin, groomed, prepared to lead and steer and direct and instruct, all the while eating warm baked cheesecake prepared for me by my house-keeper. These are the crumbs offered to me, along with tickets for musicals, dinners at Maxim's, trips in hot-air balloons, cruises on the Thames, for the stress, for the erosion of my sleep, for the thumping of my blood-pressure, for my loss of connection with losers like you. I understand myself perfectly. I do not have to search for reason or meaning or why or what or how. I know who I am and what I do.

'I own a prestige apartment facing the sparkle of the river, with south-facing views, a private car park, porter, video security, entry phone, swimming pool and a sauna to nurture my health, which is after all my wealth. I am given all this for good reason. I am valued; I am an irresistible proposition to men in parliaments and tycoons on committees and entrepreneurs of all kinds; my condom case bulges with the promise of liaison and adventure. I am the new pioneer; the great adventure of my generation is to destabilize everything and everyone.

'In my prestige apartment I am Madame de Sade. My phone never stops ringing; it is my Beethoven, speaking into it is oral sex, my shining black cock, I press buttons, phone up New York every evening, find out how the markets close, and sometimes, when Eduardo goes down on me, I wrap the cord around his neck until he begs me for mercy. If he survives, we go out to eat, or see another musical, or go to the first night of a movie, or the opening of an exhibition. I have a very special kind of love play, my instruments are straps and straddles and bulls and bears and strangles and strategies and bells and bonds and whistles. I play my own and other people's destruction silkily and easily. I calculate crashes; I am a whore in the marketplace, I do a lotta rough trade.

'I don't dream. I fuck and hit the pillow and sleep as if I've died. Under my bathrobe I am covered in bruises. My lovers and I trace each other's scars with fingers that touch the keyboard and make a volcano anywhere in the world we want to destroy, we like to abuse and use each other, it keeps us on our toes. I hate them and they hate me, this is our liberation. Yesterday I dug my nails into the flesh of a young dealer from Berlin, he came in the back seat of his Golf GTI, sperm and cocaine all over his seat covers, testimony to our wild afternoon in the maze of an underground car park, impaled on each other in fumes and brief ecstasy – yes, we have planes to catch and our pilots are waiting for us. Last week I fucked a computer millionaire, a high-flying technical whizzo; he programmed me and I flew until we both crashed into the leather of his swivel chair, screaming. We are exhausted, wide awake, berserk, invincible. And we, Lapinski, have won the moral freedom to wound. We dabble our bodies and minds and energy and money in the soils and lakes and seas and mountains of the world. We own the world.'

The bottle of sweet sherry bobs up and down on the water near where The Innocents are sharing a packet of crisps. She spreads her long white fingernails, fingers taut so they look like claws. They watch a Mercedes speed past them, and at that moment the girl thinks she can see twenty red parrots, wings on fire, fly into the sun, and the boy thinks he can see a rhino poke its horn through the moon.

The Banker pulls into a petrol station. She is electric, possessed. The taste of the salmon is still in her mouth; she spits, opens a Diet Pepsi, eats chocolate, smokes a cigarette, gargles with the Pepsi. She says, 'Fuckwit fuckwit fuckwit . . .' Her dress sticks to her body; she seems to be sweating and shivering at the same time. The garage attendant rubs his eyes. With her American Express card she buys a hundred gallons of petrol, which she demands be loaded into her car, the boot, the back and front seat, and on the roof. He does this for her in a daze. She crashes the car into a wall, buckling the front of the Mercedes, starts it again, her hands covered in blood and glass from the shattered windscreen. This time she crashes past the barrier in the zoo car park.

When my hand got mashed in the meat machine, all I remember is the panic in the women's eyes as they bent over me. And then the Alsatians began to bark. Dizzy and dripping I thought perhaps I am a late-twentieth-century saint after all? Saint Martha of the Frozen Hamburger. What is described as an Industrial Accident is my left hand guillotined somewhere below the wrist and minced with British beef. This means a whole batch of hamburgers will consist of me. Customers will buy my flesh in a sesame bun with pickle. They will sit in buses and not even know that we have all started to eat each other.

I am not in pain. My arm is in plaster. My friends take it in turn to brush my hair. Every time my father sees me his eyes fill and he has to leave the room. I used to paint my fingernails orange – they looked like a shoal of tropical fish. I am losing parts of my self. Literally. If you have hands you might as well do something intelligent or gentle with them. When I was a girl I liked to hold the baby frogs that jumped from the pond on to my wrist, but I never kissed one to turn it into a prince and I never made a wish in case my wish did not come true. I wish I had made a wish. That is my wish.

The jagged lifeline I stared at so often in the palm of my hand is gone, so I will have to invent a tale without it. I predict a wonderful future for us all. You will meet the love of your life on a bridge in July, your children will be healthy and happy and never have to beg on trains in January, there will always be enough rain to water the crops in August, bees will never become extinct in April, libraries will be open twenty-four hours in May, no one will drill for oil under your house in November and everyone will be educated in February. That leaves March, June, September, October, December for other stuff to happen.

A rope is being strung from two telegraph poles above the zoo. First it is slack and then it gets tighter. Two ladders sway against the hour before dawn. The Anorexic Anarchist looks down. She is starving and her lips are parched. She tests the rope with her toe. The Banker opens the boot of her car. She carries two of the petrol cans into the zoo, runs back to the car, takes out another two, does this again and again until they are spread out like metal corpses on the turf; the spikes of her heels sink into the mud but she does not take them off, she just keeps running to the car and back again, the beating of her heart a small earthquake that shakes early-morning London. The llama and Freddie sleep on. When Freddie wakes up he sees The Banker in her charcoal silk and stilettos carrying petrol cans and piercing them with a car aeriel. Her hands are bleeding. He rubs his eyes.

The monkeys begin to shriek, gathering their children, calling out to other animals, burying their heads under their arms, nuzzling and nudging against each other; the gibbons make loud whooping calls that echo through the city, into nightclubs and cinemas and traffic jams; the call is 65 million years old, it slithers under the foundations of buildings and rests there, it is answered in the dense forests of the gibbons' origin, it breaks the windows of the local police station.

Twenty policemen put on their boots, jump into a van, and head for a well-known pub where they think 'the trouble' comes from; they want to smash the sound with truncheons. The van smells of frightened animals, fists, rubber, uniforms and peppermints. The Banker disappears into the aquarium trailing blood from her cut hands, into the aviary and reptile house. Freddie discovers he has an erection as he watches her pour petrol through the bars of cages, splash it through every gap she can find, he watches her run for what seems like miles, in circles and zigzags, a silver streak of fury and sweat and . . . roses . . . and a will whose pulse beats harder than the elephants' stamping feet as they lift up their trunks (at the same time the policemen lift up their truncheons) and bellow (just as three young boys hit in the stomach bellow), ears spread out to the sky. The panda who has fathered twins in Madrid and Washington spits out bamboo, thumps his own belly and tries to die. He watches the giraffe become a tower of flames and collapse into itself, ankles broken, tongue hanging out, the seven bones of its neck bowing down, one by one, curving into the earth. The folds of the elephants' skin crumple as the rings of time within it burn; some roll on their backs in the mud to put out the flames; one sits in a pool of water. The lion sees the strange sight of fire over water and roars into the dream he once had, under the acacia tree. As the flames grow and animals butt their heads against walls and bars and each other, the zoo becomes a museum of murmuring lit up by a thousand eyes, and in them Freddie can see himself; he is so aroused he can hardly stand up. Birds spread their wings of fire and try to fly but there is nowhere to fly to; they die in a ball of flames in mid-air, colliding into each other, scattering feathers and seeds. The rhinoceros from Java also attempts to fly; he digs his horn into the earth so that his body is in the air for one miraculous second until the horn breaks and he becomes a putrid hulk, a smouldering monster pointing its broken ivory stub at an invisible moon. The Banker's fingers are hot and articulate, her eyes water but she does not fumble or flinch or lose her balance; she sets fire to the litter bins as if she has been rehearsing for this all her life. She looks around her. There is nothing left of the chief gorilla except his liver which lies burning on the floor of the cage like some joke sacrifice to a wayward god. The one kangaroo that manages to jump out of her allotment runs straight into the litter bin where she falls, whimpering amongst soft drink cans and chocolate wrappers. Many of the animals are unconscious from the smell of petrol and burning flesh alone. In the aquarium the tanks shatter and fish who took so many years to fly (unlike the heavy ostrich who tried to take off in one moment of panic and broke its wings) by developing the habit of jumping to enlarge their fins, now jump straight into the flames. The eels, which when old and sexually mature grow darker, the small fish hibernating at the bottom of the tanks, all fall into the fire, a cluster of tiny scaly stars; the sting-rays spew out poison and writhe in flames that burn purple and black, the silvery-brown spotted piranha sizzles in its own oil, the fish with eggs in their mouths drop them into the flames. Outside, the last of the elephants rolls on his back, legs in the air.

The llama desperately tries to turn herself into water. She becomes earth, sawdust, stones, but this is not enough to put out the fire inside The Banker; her desire is to destroy and it is hard to break desire. No matter how hard she tries, the llama cannot do it.

She becomes The Poet. Her black boots are covered in ash, her hair singed. She watches the leopards standing on their hind legs clawing at the sky, absorbs the image and tries to reshape it. She changes herself into contempt, remorse, love – and finally salt.

Freddie stares at The Banker. She is vomiting over her stilettos. He stands up and walks through the flames towards her. As the smell of burning flesh fills his lungs and makes him retch, he spits on his little finger, moistens the blisters on The Banker's lips, and presses his tongue into the burning furnace of her mouth.

I can smell burning. I'm glad my flat is insured. The sky is on fire. I dreamt I was on fire and fell from the sky into the sea. As the water filled my ears, a voice said 'You are the Dirty Young Man of Europe,' and then I realized I was shitting in the sea, it was pouring out of me, gallons of it, and I was screaming 'SAVE ME,' the sea turning brown and I was drowning in my own shit. And then a blue marbled whale swam towards me, came to save me, but as it came closer it began to flounder in the stuff coming out of me. I prefer swimming pools. At least you know what's on the bottom.

Duke is cringing under the chair, whimpering. He did this once before under the bed of a lady I was having my way with and it turned out he could smell a dead budgie – I saw it tucked into a shoe when I dragged him out. I like it better in the car – we've fucked through three massacres together, rain, the wipers going backwards, doner kebab and a thousand cigarettes afterwards to set me up for the day to come and the days after that. The sky is thick with smoke. Hitler didn't get us out – Duke and I are staying put.

Tomorrow is always another day because you can always buy something. To date I own a car phone, microwave, video, calculator that is also a diary/radio, tea maker that is also a radio, bicycle machine, vacuum to get rid of the hairs in my car, shower radio, cassette player that is also a clock/television/radio, compact disc player and recently I bought myself another Ansaphone which is also a clock and a photocopier. When I made the message to leave to callers I got Duke to bark three times by standing on his tail. Days, weeks go by and there are often no messages on the machine – I thought it would change my life, that it would be full of people trying to contact me. Wanting things is like being tortured. You're open to suggestion and your resistance is low. So the torturer beats you senseless and says, 'You need gold taps on your bath don't you?' and you say *yes*. And then he says, 'What you really need is a Cornish pasty up your arse, isn't that right?' and you say *yes yes I need a Cornish pastry up my arse*. I am more needy than I've ever been. Am I the torturer or the tortured?

In sleep I find myself in the belly of that blue marbled whale frolicking in the sea . . . and then the whale heaves, begins to vomit me up . . . thrashes about until I am thrown out of the centre of its belly. For ever.

The anorexic anarchist walks above the flames of The Banker's boredom on her tightrope. A black cat with a pearl collar sits on her shoulder staring at her sister lioness burn below. She takes three steps, her bare feet as slow and as sure as a tortoise; she pauses and breathes deeply; the heat is almost unbearable. Thick coils of smoke circle her head like a halo. On the seventh step she balances herself with her arms, fingers outstretched, dripping with sweat, and says

derangement is the subversion of order
i am deranged
i am starving
i have taken the pain of the world into my self
i have not walked on water but i have walked above fire

She loses her balance, stumbles, adjusts herself with flailing smoke-blackened arms. Her palms are blistered. She takes another three steps, her green hair blowing in the putrid wind.

The Poet stands in her black boots on a mound of ash. Her belly heaves. She staggers out on to the city streets, blinking away the fur in her eyes, itching from the ash that has fallen on discarded washing machines and broken chairs in the gutter, walks for hours in zigzags through the middle of roads and down alleys, she walks and walks, comes to what looks like a bridge of black bone, trips over the sprawled legs of a boy and a girl. The Innocents are sleeping under a blanket that has absorbed the smell of dying animals, their heads resting on a white DIAL A PIZZA BOX. The girl clutches a smaller white box to her breast and in it, neatly arranged, are the ten white fake fingernails, the boy nuzzling into her neck, spiked hair sticky with tea leaves: he is dreaming of Jerusalem, which he pronounces Jar-oos'a-lam, where he finds wild sage growing in the cracks of the wailing wall; he wants to find water to boil and brew the sage to give to the girl who is murmuring softly, sometimes drowned by the trains, 'No babies . . . I don't want babies . . . no babies.'

Freddie withdraws his tongue from The Banker's mouth. He says, 'I find your fire sexy, Miss.' Their shoes are sticky with vomit. 'Why do you find me sexy, son of a bitch?' She slaps his face and neck and ears. 'Why Why Why?' Freddie catches her hands – which are tearing the skin on his face – with his own hands, and squeezes them until the knuckles go white.

'Because I too want to act on my worst desires, to love my wickedness. I have fought this tendency in myself but now I want to give up the good fight. I want to glory in the truth of my worst nightmares. I want to live on adrenalin and deceit, to pluck the feathers off niceness, to drip scalding wax on my old utopian visions, to stick my fingers up at newly-weds . . . at rosy optimism . . . I want to fuck you in the flames. If the world is your playground I want to play with you; teach me to play. I will be your disciple. I want you to be my teacher, to scold and whip and kiss and suckle me. I want you to offer me a dangerous future. You are the woman I have yearned for all my life. I have found you and do not fear our difference. I have found the hidden jagged edges of myself in you, found forbidden desire in you,

95

found my meanest self in you, in your womanly form . . . and
I want you.'

The Banker screws up her eyes, watches the flames throw
shadows over the golden contours of his body.' Come here then.
Fuck this top goddess in the flames and I will be your chair-
woman.' She lifts up her torn silk dress and tells him how she
wants him to move.

'I am the first transsexual who's performed her own operation.
I am a man-woman, and you, Freddie . . . I see you have been
feminized . . . learnt the language of women I despise. I killed that
woman in myself long ago. Drowned it in my husband's semen,
drowned my disgusting neediness in the silicone heart of a
machine better than my body. I pay no attention to the moon of
blood and backache. I stopped all that long ago. I am totally in
control. I have no appetite for love. None at all. I am love's arson-
ist, burnt it out of myself, where it was is now a smouldering field
full of stubble. I am beautiful and brutal, soft and hard; a myth in
a technological age. I have mistressed that age and become its
master with my womanly contours, hairless skin, perfect breasts
and tears. I woo seduce confuse and legislate . . . SUSTAIN IT
BADBOY OR I'LL BREAK YOUR LEGS WITH MY
WILL . . . HARDER HARDER HARDER . . . Inside my
womanly structure I can achieve what no man can even hope for.
I am witch, mother, sister, mistress, maiden, whore, nun, princess. I
am raping you with archetypes you yourself invented . . . listen to
the peacocks howl like hyenas, who would have thought it of such
a pretty bird . . . COME COME YOU BASTARD COME!'

She pulls down her dress and asks Freddie to brush her hair.

He walks behind her, tenderly untangling knots, smoothing, caressing, stroking. She smiles. He puts on his trousers, limp and breathless and happy. Her breath, which smells of petroleum, is his wind of liberation. He feels abused, soiled, burnt, ecstatic.

She says, 'Breakfast. Croissants, coffee, orange juice, newspapers. I'll pay.' He takes her arm and they walk through the flames to the car park. She drives him to her favourite café where a waiter guides them to The Banker's private table, under an arch of stone. They can hear fire engines, police sirens, the babble of journalists, the flashlights of photographers.

'So you see,' says The Banker, dipping her croissant into her cappuccino, crumbs on her glossed lips, she pauses while nostalgic Muzak from a war-time movie washes gently over the walls and little baskets of warm bread rolls. 'We will inherit the earth.' She watches the waiter slice oranges and put them in the juice extractor. 'How many pigs have you got in your mouth then?' She smiles at Freddie who blinks and bites into his bacon sandwich.

'Yes, Lapinski,' says The Poet, waving her hand in the direction of the café with arches and domes and a striped canopy, 'they will die stuffed and empty and we will die half full.' Tonight, the moths that circle the light of my lamp like a wreath have wings that are singed at the tips. My cat Krupskaya seems to be dizzy. The pearls on her collar have melted and every time she tries to walk she falls down. When I tickle her under the chin she begins to wash her ears and prance about like a tsarina with a hangover. The Poet requests another cup of tea and a Jammie Dodger, a biscuit she is partial to way before and after the acceptable age to like Jammie

97

Dodgers, those ages being seven and seventy. She is not particularly grateful which is a relief because being grateful can be quite tiring.

She says, 'A friend of mine recently lost her hand on the meatbelt, you know . . . better to lose your marbles than your hand, don't you think? In my next metamorphosis I'm going to be a Professor of Madness and I'll say to my students, If you want to know what health is, first you must know what sickness is: go and look at the way desks are arranged in offices and ask every Senior Manager and CEO what kinds of strategies they have in place to make their employees feel uneasy and ask career politicians what it is they do not believe in and ask the pornography industry what it is they are selling and ask farmers if there's any reason why hens should be able to move freely and ask the pharmaceutical industry if it's ever thought of bribing doctors to use its products and ask the floggers and hangers if their parents were kind to them and ask the present what's it's got to do with the past – and if it's true that hope does not die last, it dies first, does anybody know where the bodies are buried?'

She stands up and thanks me for the Jammie Dodger.

In another part of London, Jerry sings

> *'for-give . . . me*
> *for-give . . . me*
> *for-give . . . me'*

And Eduardo joins in

'per-do-no
per-do-no
per-do-no.'

In the little restaurant which pays my rent and where people eat lamb stew and read newspapers in a variety of languages, the woman with the broken Chinese umbrella sits opposite me and says, 'Lapinski, my friend is dying.' I pour salt on to the aubergines I have just sliced and she watches it turn the flesh of the vegetable brown. 'At the hospital, by his bed, we no longer talk about what is right or wrong. We talk about parks and we talk about bread.' Her eyelashes are silver, her cheekbones sharp. 'He loves a particular park in Paris and how the hedges are sculpted and we pretend we will go back to visit it with two baguettes in our rucksack.' She smiles and the sun shines on her see-through hands, the veins a nest of blue snakes. 'I am clearing out his room for him. It is not his personal correspondence that makes me feel strange – it is his objects. A little horse made from lead. A duck's egg. A candle in the shape of a cactus. They seem suspended in time, like a miracle.' She take the aubergines and squeezes them in her hands until their juice trickles into a saucer. Her left palm is covered in little white seeds. After a while she says, 'Why the silence?'

I tell her how my father, a docker, always found time to take me to the public baths where he held my wrists and floated me out into the middle of the pool. So I would not be frightened of the deep, he made little boats out of paper and sailed them a short distance away from me. In this way he taught me how to swim. And how my mother changed from the clothes she wore to make engines for tractors, into the sparkling taffeta skirt with spangles and sequins, glittering as she danced for the sheer fun of getting dizzy; and how she would eat beetroot which she loved more than chocolate, and leave little red kiss marks on my cheeks and hands. She nods and smiles. 'No one can read our thoughts even if they think they can.'

For some reason her words make me remember the helicopter I saw in the sky the night before. From the thirteenth floor of The Poet's high-rise flat. How it had a yellow beam shooting down, searching for someone. In gardens, down roads, through the windows of houses. Although it was unlikely, I had felt scared in case they were searching for me and I did not know what I had done. But the most frightening thing of all was I felt they did not know what I had done either.

Swallowing Geography

And I say to any man or woman, Let your soul stand cool and
    composed before a million universes.
Do I contradict myself?
Very well then I contradict myself,
(I am large, I contain multitudes.)

Walt Whitman, Song of Myself

I

The Tadpole Fields

'When you feel fear, does it have detail or is it just a force?' The gold filling in Gregory's front tooth shines into J. K.'s eye. 'I can't hear you.'

They are sitting in a bar surrounded by mirrors etched with the Eiffel Tower at Roissy airport, Paris. Brand names like Segafredo, Perrier, Dior, Kronenbourg 1664, Chanel spin like planets above them. The large blonde Californian waitress slams two cocktails down on the table.

'They're killers,' she says.

'It is as if Paris is muffled. I hear it at low volume.'

J.K. says nothing because these days Gregory's voice is very quiet, as if frightened to let it out of his big body. She catches odd words like nausea, chestpain, The Baltic States, mother, father, aspirin, and sometimes she catches his eye.

'Look at the inscription in this book.'

She moves closer to the secret in his body that tames his voice.

It is an old volume of short stories printed in 1941 on thin transparent paper.

'Leave this book at the Post Office when you have read it, so that men and women in the services may enjoy it too.'

The day before, they walked to Pigalle in silence, arm in arm, stopping to watch transvestite whores lean against cars and walls, put on lipstick, smoke cigarettes, call out to men passing by, their steamy drugged gaze settling on this man and that man and then somewhere else.

'What kind of cultural virus taught those boys to stick their hips out like that, and pout and press their breasts across the other side of the road?' Gregory says.

'Do you fancy them?'

'They're gorgeous. I like that one over there with the long black plait . . . it comes down to his knees, can you see . . . in the hat with the red feather.'

COME AND TALK TO ME! It is an eerie staccato voice. The voice of cigarette advertisements, fierce sun, a two-bit bar with dead flies on the floor. They turn round to see they are standing outside a pinball arcade, CASINO spelt in coloured lightbulbs above the door. COME AND TALK TO ME! The yankee growling voice comes from a silver and chrome machine. On its screen a square muscled man jumps up and down in a computerized urban landscape of skyscrapers and highways. Hands in raincoat pocket, jaw jerking to one side, he drawls again, COME AND TALK TO ME!

Gregory nudges J.K.'s arm. 'Well, listen to the man, let's take up his invitation.' He puts ten francs in the slot.

HOW YA DOING? says the man. TYPE SOMETHING INTO THE KEYBOARD AND I WILL RESPOND. The screen whirs as the urban cowboy crosses his arms and leans towards them.

'It's in English.'

'Well, tell him how you are.'

Gregory turns to face the man. He puts another ten francs into the machine and spreads out his fingers. Pink and blue bulbs flash above him.

Do your lips burn up when kissed right? Let me kiss 'em baby. Let me let me let me. I would like to fuck you. I would like to make you happy. How do you like to be touched? On the aeroplane over here, the air hostess demonstrated various ways of surviving an aircrash. She said we must blow on a whistle to draw attention to ourselves. Don't you think that is a little narcissistic? If everyone in the everyday of their lives who wanted to draw attention to themselves blew a whistle where would we be? What do you do to make people love you? I do cheap things to make people like me. I make them feel more important than they are and flatter them and when someone makes me a great cocktail I take a sip and shout DRAGONFLIES! In England I light my cigarettes with matches made in Yugoslavia. The picture on the box is of 'Scenic Cornwall' and shows a number of signposts on the edge of a cliff. One of them says THE FALKLANDS 8109 and the other says AUSTRALIA 170001. I tell you this because when I was a boy I collected stamps. It was my way of naming places and conquering the world. A stamp is a small picture. So I had lots of small pictures of the world. Madagascar, China, Mexico, Argentina, Egypt. A kind of virtual reality.

What's your name, my sweet? Is it Johnny or Sam or Brett? I'd like to go down on you and for you to talk to me about football and religion and hamburgers and beauty and death and what it feels like to come. Were you bullied at school? When you were a teenager did you spend hours in your bedroom changing your clothes? Did you save up to buy the boots and shirts other kids had? What kind of Darwinian programmed you? Do you want to change yourself in any way? Like speak in a deeper voice or have a different nose? Do you feel safe in this world? Or do you feel alone and scared? What kind of gadgets do you have in your home? Do they comfort you? Baby do you sometimes feel glum? Baby take care of yourself. Oh baby I'd like to stroke you and whisper things to you and make you not have fear.

Honey, I want to tell you about a train I took to Kiev with my bit of squeeze. We made love just as we got near Chernobyl and the loudspeakers in our carriage played a kind of lament to mark the tragedy of the nuclear accident. In some way it seemed to mark all tragedy ever. The cries of our lovemaking as we passed infected cattle, children with shaved heads playing by the railway tracks and the eerie stillness of deformed trees were the only sound, snow falling, he and I sweating in each other's arms and honey we were, at that moment, without fear. The high-rise blocks of flats we stayed in were called The Sleeping Region. I was brought up in a block like that in London. As a kid we lived on tins of beans and meatballs and hated to sleep because we were frightened. Darling, do you sleep sweet and easy and deep? Does someone sleep beside you? Breathing into the pillow next to you and you wake up first and feel them there and it's just so great that they're there and you know very soon they will wake too and you will move closer and kind of pull in the beginning of a new day together? In Kiev I opened tins of crab meat and caviar bought with hard currency and we slept easy. We slept easy and there was a famine outside. The circus played every night in Kiev − an old man sitting next to me made a joke about eating the cats and horses after the show. Are you happy with your life, my sweet? The man said, 'You can always tell a tourist, their eyes don't know where they're going. Here everyone knows where they're going.' Do you know where you're going baby? Is it a good place? Something to write home about? Is home a good place? Or just somewhere to return to?

Are you pleased to open your eyes in the morning? What do you see? Do you like what you see? If you hate it do you feel you have any power to change it for something else? Oh my love, let me call you that – My Love – let us imagine what that means, you and I liplocked some place in the American South, perhaps where the Klan lynched our brothers? You and I in a motor on the highway making plans for the future. The radio is on and we hear the Soviet Union has come apart and then there are some ads for Pepsi and bagel chips, and back to a war in Yugoslavia, nationalisms and internationalisms, an election in Great Britain, refugees crossing mountains looking for a country to feed them, a jingle for vitamin capsules, and all the time we are hot for each other, through all this world news we just want to be in each other's pants, and we pull in for gas and I'm saying, No baby don't light a cigarette right now, wait till we pull out and anyhow we'll check into a motel soon. Hey Brett, I'm Imagining America! It's all from movies and magazines, I'm fumbling to make you America. I'm fumbling to make you and unmake you. Abe Lincoln on your dollar bills – IN GOD WE TRUST – pastrami and gas and tacos and beer bought with his image, he's the guy that keeps the wheels turning. I'm stuffing chocolate into your mouth and baby … you're so hard, so hard honey … you're all fired up and I'm talkin' dirty, I'm talking physical, I'm talking politics and dontcha just love it, got my fingers in your armpit and you're sweating bad. I want you too baby I want you too. Y'know that Springsteen song … oh baby I'd drive all night again jus' to buy you a pair of shoes? Well I would. I'd drive to hell and back jus' to make you love me.

How do you love? Do you keep it quiet and put it all in your fingertips or do you say words? What are your lovewords baby? What if the United States came apart? Would God come apart too and the stone pillars of the Abe Lincoln memorial crumble and statues of George Washington be torn up from squares of green, watered by sprinklers? Torn up by crane and bulldozer?

Now I am imagining Switzerland, Brett. I can see snow and stripped pine floors and coffee shops and cream cakes and blond people tinkling little silver spoons against their cups. I see children in nursery schools that are heated, very warm and very clean and their little snow boots lined up against the wall and gloves sewn into their coat pockets. I can't imagine you there, Brett. I'm trying to see a teacher bent over your shoulder while you draw your mother and father and the house you live in and giant flowers – but I just can't vision you in Switzerland skiing and eating chocolate. You'd probably shoot up in your chalet, lie down in your shorts under the skylight, arms folded behind your neck looking up at the stars dreaming of home and bourbon and cookies and having a haircut. You see how I'm making you up, same as Switzerland and America? Does it feel like it fits you? Have you made me up too? Am I some kind of English faggot crazy for boys, cruising into my adult life in black leather under strobe and sonic boom of city discos? There's such a lot to talk about baby, just you and me, man to man. Did you hear about the man who went to a psychologist and said, Doctor I think I'm a dog, and the doctor said, we'll soon sort that out, now get on the couch. And the man said, but I'm not allowed. Well I'm inviting you to be whatever you like sweetheart, I'm listening to you, I'm listening to everything you want to be and were not allowed. Brett, I'm saying make yourself up for me baby, have as many goes as you like, be the man you always wanted to be, and I'll be the man that lets you. Brett, life is long dontcha think? When you tot up the hours and days and months it's a lot of time. How much of that time have you felt precious? I want to make you feel precious, my treasure, my lovestuff. Have you ever driven across a city you don't know very well and you're alone? It's night and you're lost. Had too many beers in some bar where they look at you as if you're an extraterrestrial immigrant and somewhere else, in another city, there's someone who loves you and you imagine them looking at you in this bar now, checking you out, what shoes you've put on today and what you're drinking and what kind of mood you're in? And you want to say to the people in this bar who think you're some kind of weirdo blown in to undo them – I am connected to the same things as you y'know – I have people who love me and I watch TV and I have a birthday and I brush my teeth and I'm not always like this, eating crap pizza alone and lost with this look in my eyes. And then you get into the car and none of the street signs makes sense, and you just cry. Brett, have you done this? And you think of all the people you've jilted meanly and all the people who dumped you, and your pockets are full of old bills and tickets and you turn over all the secrets you carry inside you?

SOUNDS LIKE YA NEED SOME HELP! The handsome urban cowboy uncrosses his thick arms and takes out a gun. Suddenly he jumps on to a moving car, shoots, jumps off the car and thrashes a man across the head with his gun, runs, leaps over a motorcycle, crouches, shoots, climbs up a skyscraper, hangs on with one hand, shoots with the other, kicks a man chasing him off the building, shoots him in mid-air, dives through a pane of glass, shoots two three four five six other men, runs on to the roof of the skyscraper, flags down a helicopter, gets into it and pours bullets into the heart of the city – a loop of shooting and dying and dying and shooting and shooting and dying and then the voice says . . . COME AND TALK TO ME . . .

'I can't hear you, Greg,' J.K. says in the airport lounge.

'I know.'

'Have you seen a doctor?'

'Yeah.'

They finish their cocktails in silence.

'Look.'

J.K. opens her mouth and shows him the bloody gap where a tooth should be.

Gregory stares at her. Black flecks float in his green eyes.

'What happened?'

'I got slugged.'

'By who?'

'My mother. Knocked a tooth out.'

'Lillian?'

Their flight number comes up on the screen and they walk to the gate for take-off.

'Tell me about getting slugged.'

The aeroplane shudders and they put on their seat belts.

2

The Terrible Rages of Lillian Strauss

Her mother comes towards her carrying a black suitcase. J.K. walks three paces, takes the bag from her mother's hands and says, when I walked towards you, something inside me walked too. Some beast that has taken up residence inside me, that inhabits the colony of my interior, that has decided to inhabit me against my will, walked with me towards you. It lifted up each of its four legs and walked the three paces with me. The petrol winds from the Texaco petrol station wake her up blowing through the open window, and instead of birds, the panicky whir of the car-wash. Later, on her balcony, J.K. sees the camellia she planted last year has blossomed. One pink bud, opening and opening, just as she in sleep is opening and her mother sliding in behind her eyes.

Lillian Strauss is J.K.'s mother.

Her mother says, in Singapore every evening at six o'clock, a tray of drinks would be brought in by a servant. Gin and tonic, an ice bucket, lemon and bitters. We would drink until we went to bed, dropped on cotton pillows. Your uncle had a grog's blossom for a nose, purple-veined, a great bloom. J.K. thinks of her camellia blossoming on a concrete balcony in a poor part of London, opening and opening.

Her mother, in another poor part of London, walks the streets in one of her rages. She is mouthing words to lamp-posts and parked cars; she is weeping and she is drunk. Her husbands have left her, her children have left her, her beauty has left her, she is filling the holes of absence with gin-scented tears and, like the suitcase, she wants to be carried, lifted into a sweeter present.

The wind hurls plastic bags up from the gutter and into the air. They fly like strange torn birds battered in a gale. Sheets of metal and bits of scaffolding fall from buildings on to the pavement. Mothers clutch their children and hurry home. The sky is the colour of dead fish. A man shuffles towards J.K., losing one of his slippers on the way. Beery breath, face much too close to hers, he whispers, 'Little woman, you have blood under your crotch,' and limps off into the swirling litter, a deranged prophet on the edge of the desert, walking into a swarm of locusts.

Lillian Strauss is planting red pokers in her garden. She digs and digs. Sometimes she buries bottles in her garden, binliners full of bottles; vodka, whisky, gin, wine, and once as a joke, an SOS, tucked into a very special bottle of malt whisky, a secret note for someone to find in the future. 'My red-hot pokers will bloom,' says Lillian Strauss, 'even in this bloody English soil.' And then she says to J.K., who hands her airmail letters so she can write to her sister in Singapore, 'You are a fool even though you are cunning and let me tell you this dear, you're hardly a matinee idol.'

'We're going to celebrate us in style J.K.'

Ebele orders two glasses of champagne and a plate of chips. Seven foot tall, in a suit and little red fez, he shows her his shoes. They are full of holes which he's stuffed with newspaper so he creaks every time he walks. His wrists jingle with bracelets and they are in a bar in Oxford, surrounded by pale young couples eating salmon cakes; somewhere, bells are ringing, ringing through the Muzak and neat pastel blouses.

J.K. dips a chip into a puddle of ketchup, circling it round and round, smiling and looking away, and then looking straight into his black eyes – just as the Muzak drawls, 'Loooovin' you whah whah ooooooooooooh.'

Ebele so big, the glass of champagne small in his hand, in his beautiful wide-palmed hand, bells ringing through his fingers, as he creaks and jingles, rocks backwards and forwards on his chair. He tells her he is a twin and how his twin brother died at birth, weighing two pounds. He, Ebele, weighed eleven pounds, and when the cord was cut, his brother died next to him, thin and sickly, and he a giant baby freak screaming on a slab in Sierre Leone, nose to nose with his starved dead brother.

'I felt a murderer y'know . . . for years after, so when I come to the West, first thing I do is look up a book to see how twins lie in the womb.' Ebele scoops up a handful of chips into his mouth and sips his champagne as if it were Guinness. 'I learn it was my mouth that was wrapped round the food supply innit.' His mouth is full of potato. 'Yeh. But the spirit of my twin brother is always with me. My baby brother. He is my lucky charm. When things go wrong in life I feel him with me. He is the boy who stops the planes I fly in from crashing.'

He claps his hands and the tassels on his fez shiver under the air conditioner.

'My hands feel so weak today. Look at my fingers. They're like spaghetti.'

Lillian Strauss has very thin earlobes and very thin lips. She has a Biro in her hand and while she talks she doodles. The word Aristotle appears twice, and underneath it, a tortoise carrying a little red flower in its mouth. That's my insignia, she says. Like people have tartans, I have tortoises. Her daughter laughs. In response to the laughter Lillian Strauss sketches a young girl holding a long-eyelashed cat by the lead. Good night angel, she says, I can't drive you home because of my night blindness, and while she describes what it's like not to be able to see in the dark, J.K. looks at her mother's collection of tigers. They are arranged in little groups all over the house, striped heads and glassy eyes. Good night angel, she says, and her voice is panicked, breathless, just as it always is when she expresses affection. And then when everything seems okay, the words Good night angel, the puckering of lips to kiss, there is a sea change. Lillian Strauss says, you hate all my family, you don't want to know about my childhood in Singapore, you think I am a w.a.s.p., you ignore half your blood, and she begins to write in the same biro, a 'hymn of hate' to her daughter. The tigers look on. They look straight into J.K., yowling great cries into her heart.

There is a beast inside J.K. It is a mammoth, frozen in ice. It inhabits the colony of her interior and sometimes it stirs. While her mother writes the hymn of hate, she can feel it nudge its big ugly head against the ice. When her mother says, 'I love you so much,' it lies down again, and rests. 'You are going away again,' says Lillian Strauss. 'Good riddance.'

Starlings fill the sky. They circle a large whitewashed mansion with green shutters raised above the bay. Scarlet blooms grow in turquoise pots and trees bend in the breeze inside the walls of the garden. There is shade in that garden. And a hammock strung between lemon trees. There is health in that garden. Cool walls and birdsong. I'd get to look young in that place. I'd come home to rest in that place. I'd stop running, running through airports and railway stations, running through European cities looking for rooms and coffee and company and comfort. I would stop running away from this beast inside me. We would rest here and stop being frightened of each other.

Lillian Strauss has sold her house, sold her car ('four hundred pounds and it's yours'), sold a carpet, sold some silver cutlery, sold a bronze buddha, and moved to another suburb in London. She drinks a bottle of dry white wine at 11 a.m. and says to her daughter, I want a sea funeral, I want to be buried at sea. J.K.

says, 'You've always liked the sea,' and gives her a clay tiger she has brought back from Spain. By 1 p.m. her mother has finished the wine and is making scones. She is not a scone-making mother, but her mother made scones and she is trying to remember the recipe. She breaks lumps of butter into the flour and says, this is to let them breathe. The smell of scones cooking fills the kitchen and Lillian Strauss folds her arms over her soiled cardigan. She stares at her new tiger with dull eyes.

'I saw a park full of picnicking women yesterday afternoon. Young mothers and their children. They were picnicking on rugs and they were happy. I wanted to buy cherries and for us, you and me, to sit in the park and soak up the sun. I wanted to be as easy, as free and easy as those young mothers when I was a young mother.' She stops and her cheeks are burning. 'You have that horrible look on your face. You're always plotting.' Lillian Strauss is in one of her rages. She opens the oven and with her bare hands takes out the baking tin. Half the scones are sweet and half sizzle with melted cheese. She plunges her hands into them, tears them apart and throws them against the walls of the kitchen, her burnt hands writhing like snakes through the bone-white grass of her discontent.

Ebele brings J.K. one of his paintings for her birthday: an orange hand, its palm laced with henna, similar to Indian brides at weddings.

'Count the fingers,' he says.

'Six.' She smiles. 'Six orange fingers.'

'From your alien friend. They tell me I'm an alien at the airport.' He holds up his own fingers and tells J.K. to count them.

One, two, three, four, five. She kisses his hand and then bursts into tears. Afterwards, as they walk in the park hand in hand, kicking piles of new mown grass into smaller piles, she tells him about her mother's blistered hands laced with sizzling cheese.

Lillian Strauss arrives at her daughter's house with a large tin of tomato soup and a black pudding sausage. The hem of her dress is held together with safety pins and her calves are scratched and bloody. Ha ha laughs Lillian Strauss. 'Just from the pins dear. They come undone. What did you think they were?' Her cheeks are covered in a nerve rash. She thumps the black pudding on the table.

'Guess where I got the money to buy that.'

'Where?'

'I finished the *Times* crossword and won twenty quid.'

As they eat, Lillian Strauss points to the sausage pronged on her fork.

'What's this?'

'Meat.'

'No my dear. This is congealed blood.'

She puts it in her mouth and chomps with relish.

J.K. thinks about how much she loves her mother.

The panic of the raging beast. J.K. wears a summer dress the colour of the lemons she glimpsed in the walled garden. The colour she saw standing on the wrong side of paradise. Ebele stands behind her, plaiting her hair, brushing it, smoothing it down, weaving lemon ribbons into the braids.

*

Lillian Strauss takes a hammer and thrashes the ice tray. It is six o'clock, time for gin and tonic, a little bowl of peanuts, intimacies and brittle jokes. As the gin bottle empties, her hand tightens around her glass and laughter changes to melancholy. She begins to name all the cats she has owned and how each one of them died. 'I would have liked grandchildren to get sober for,' she weeps. One day J.K. gives her a present. Five papier mâché Chinese children. Round faces and black hair. There are blossoms painted on their clothes. Lillian Strauss arranges and rearranges them on a little straw mat, and J.K. observes that her mother has no half moons on her fingernails. Just as she is thinking this, Lillian Strauss flings one of the Chinese children to the floor and stamps on it with her square brown heels. 'What you need is a good kick up the arse. It's big enough.' The papier mâché baby lies crumpled on its stomach, cheek pressed into the carpet, and on the sole of Lillian Strauss's shoe, a little hand with three broken fingers.

Her mother points to the red hot pokers thrusting out of the stony soil of her garden. 'What do you think of my red garden, J.K.?' She leans over and strokes the stem. 'Your pink camellia, my dear, is for the cowardly.' The noise of the day fades.

When Lillian Strauss turns round to face the heat and silence behind her neck, she thinks her garden is on fire. And then she sees a mouth, a massive mouth, opening, opening, until it fills the whole of her eye, a quivering thing, standing in the blaze of her red-hot pokers. She clenches her fist and thumps it into the mouth of the beast, alone with the child she created.

3
Re-imagining the Stranger

He walks in although she has no memory of leaving the door open. When she turns round to face him, he says, 'You are bare-foot, you have one tooth missing, and you are wearing a blue dress.'

'Why do you always describe me?'

Silence.

'Your lips are cracked,' she says.

They are sitting together on the sofa. It is a warm night, the heat of the day pouring in through the windows. He takes out a wad of papers from his brown leather bag, the bag travellers strap across their chests, a few essentials packed with care. A book, a pen, a bottle of orange flower water, a passport, a photo, a slab of chocolate, a wallet heavy with foreign coins.

'Currency,' he says.

'I have been thinking about strangers,' she says.

He smiles and looks out of the window.

'How a stranger never belongs to a person or to a place. He can be an insider and an outsider at the same time.'

At that moment he puts his arms around her and her eyelash touches his cracked lips.

In bed they laze about for a while and then she climbs on top of him and says, 'Tell me about zones and frontiers.' He is kissing her shoulders, his lips are cool and he is saying, 'Um . . . ooh . . . there are um naked frontiers, take off your blue dress, and there are . . . um zones you can go into and zones you can't. Do you like being touched here or here?' She considers telling him where she was born, how old she is and what she does for a living.

'What's your name?' He puts his hand on her breast.

J.K.

She notices that this time (they have only been naked once together before) he shuts his eyes when last time he kept them open. She thinks he has his eyes shut because he is feeling something he did not feel before.

'You are naked apart from three silver bracelets,' he says.

'You're describing me again.'

'That's what strangers do. When they are in an unfamiliar place they describe it.'

'We are intimate strangers,' she says.

'Yes.'

They lie side by side, heads touching as the sky deepens and shops pull down their shutters.

'Do you want a glass of German champagne?'
'Was it a present?'
'Yes.'
'Why German?'
She shrugs.
'There's a story you're not telling me. That's how you keep someone a stranger.' And then, 'HEY you've got your shoes on. How can that be? You didn't have shoes on when I arrived. When did you put them on? We've been screwing and you've kept your shoes on!'

J.K. ties up the laces.

'These aren't just any shoes. They are made for walking long distances.'

She goes to fetch the champagne and, just as they open it, she lying across his back, there is a knock on the door. She says, 'That will be Zoya. A friend of mine.'

He is shy and surprised and puts his hand into the silver curls of his hair.

'But it's late . . . it's . . .'

'She has driven one hundred and ninety miles to see me.' J.K. pulls on her blue dress and leaves him naked in her bedroom.

Zoya wears little horn-rimmed spectacles (even though her eyes have perfect vision), a mantilla comb in her hair, and carries a small spherical black suitcase.

'It's the doctor,' she guffaws. 'Where does it hurt?' Despite the humidity of this unnaturally warm night she also carries an overcoat. 'Got no love to keep me warm,' she says, and takes a pineapple out of her spherical black bag. She saws through the thick skin with a bread knife and sucks a ring of pulpy flesh. 'Those are the green plates you bought in Brixton market.' She points to a shelf above the fridge, catching the juice running down her chin with a cupped hand. The stranger walks in and strokes J.K.'s hair.

'You are wearing a blue dress, three silver bracelets, walking shoes, and you bought six green plates in Brixton market.'

Zoya adjusts her spectacles and lights a cigarette.

'Are you going to introduce us?'

Silence.

'This is J.K.,' he says.

The migrant stranger and the migrant Zoya sit together in another room while J.K. cooks. They begin to find oceans, motorways, railway lines, bus routes, facial characteristics, languages, bread, fruit, fish, jokes and musical instruments in common. When J.K. returns with plates of food and sits on a chair opposite them, she feels like a stranger.

The next evening, London is divided into two zones – by telephone. Inner and Outer, Central and Suburban. 071 and 081. The Post Office Tower celebrates by spinning laser beams into the sky. Zoya and J.K. are walking down Charlotte Street, West London, looking for a place to eat lamb kebabs.

'How can I wo-rk when the sky's so blu-e. How can I wo-rk like other wo-men do,' Zoya croons.

'I miss my family,' she says.

'You've never said that before.'

They sit down at a little café with tables and chairs sprawled on the pavement.

'It's the smell of lamb and heat.'

The waiter takes their order.

'I used to be able to speak Urdu as a child. Then this country beat it out of me. One night I got drunk in Berlin and remembered everything. I even remembered languages I didn't know I spoke! I remembered the house I grew up in, what part of the garden had shade and how I used to swill out the yard with buckets of cold water while my brothers played football. I was beside myself, babbling in tongues.' She takes off her fake spectacles, puts them into a red fake leather case and snaps it shut. 'And then I looked up into the cold grey eyes of the man sitting opposite me.'

'What man?'

'He told me he sold early Max Ernst etchings for millions of marks, all the time chasing a ribbon cut from the cheese he was eating across his plate. And then he talked about how he wanted to breed heavy horses . . .'

J.K. laughs.

'This was balm, J.K. I wanted to escape from the bloody pain sticking through my ribs, and heavy horses were just the thing. It could have been tortoises, stars, a list of rare ivy, buttonholes. He wore a crisp white shirt and citron cologne, and it was perfect, our difference was perfect. Like the Irish poet Patricia Scanlan who pushed all the grief of Belfast out of her head by writing lists of every sweet she bought as a kid at the local shop, I asked him the names and types of all the horses he wanted to breed.' She giggles. 'He told me he liked the idea of rubbing them down at 5 p.m., when they were hot and panting! And I said things like hmmmm in-neresting, like I was a B-movie cop. I think he thought I was a headcase but he couldn't resist a rapt audience. We went our separate ways and I bought you a bottle of champagne to celebrate.'

'I drank it with the stranger.'

The waiter pours wine into Zoya's glass.

'This wine is the colour of health. It's not like other wines. This is medicine.' The waiter who is still standing by Zoya's side smiles and says something to her in a language J.K. doesn't understand.

'He says he will read our coffee cups.'

'You are flowers,' he says, and disappears into the heat and bustle of the restaurant.

'I miss my family too.' J.K. sucks a long green chilli.

'But they only live a tube ride away.'

'I know.'

Someone has taken a photograph of them. A sweet peppery perfume and a blinding flash. They look up into the golden teeth of a middle-aged man, trousers belted high over his paunch, carnation in his buttonhole.

'For you, girls. Only five pounds.'

He waves the Polaroid through the air so that Zoya and J.K. can see bits of themselves developing second by second.

'Are we here yet?'

Two women sit at a small slanting table covered with a plastic cloth. One has a glass of wine between her finger and thumb, hands resting on a red spectacle case. Her shoulders are turned in towards her friend and her lips make the shape of the word 'medicine'. The other has her legs crossed, bread in hand, chilli in the other. Her cheekbones are burnt from a day in the sun and her lips have just finished making the shape of the word 'family'.

'You are here.' The photographer points to each of them on the Polaroid.

'We know we are here,' Zoya says.

He leans over and takes a toothpick from their table, tilts his head and works it into his golden teeth.

'Sometimes it's good to know where you are.'

The waiter lifts J.K.'s cup from the saucer.

'Why are you laughing?' she asks him.

'What's your name?'

'J.K.'

'I'll tell you one thing, J.K.'

'Okay.'

'You must give yourself a name.'

071 and 081 for London. The Post Office Tower lights up and J.K. stares into her cup.

He walks in although she has no memory of leaving the door open. When she turns round to face him, he says, 'You are wearing jeans and a silk halterneck.'

'You have an airmail letter in your top pocket,' she says.

It is a cold night and it is beginning to rain. J.K. is thinking, I have just left the 071 zone to come back here, to these rooms, the books on my shelves, to the fruit in my bowl, and to this man. Is that what a home is? A place to invite strangers to? He is staring at the snakeskin buckles on her shoes.

'Y'know,' she says, and he turns his body towards her. 'My name is . . .'

His gaze shifts from her eyes to the radio behind her head. 'I like it that you're just called J.K.' When he lets his eyes meet hers she sees they are frightened.

''Bye,' she says.

He tangles his fingers with her fingers.

'What are you still doing here?'

He says, 'Start again. Why don't you take off your shoes and tell me who you are.'

'You like it that I'm just called J.K.'

'Tell me who you are so I can love you properly.'

She considers these words. There are eleven walnuts in a bowl by her feet and there are eleven words for her to consider. Tell-me-who-you-are-so-I-can-love-you-properly.

'You want me to be a stranger,' he says and, for the first time ever, takes out a cigarette that smells of cloves, lights it and leans against the sofa.

'You even wear shoes in bed so you can walk away from me.'

She stands up, switches on the radio, and looks at him sitting there, in her home, too close, a coil of smoke above his silver head, airmail letter shivering in his top pocket. At that moment, the radio announces that war has broken out, and tanks are sliding through the ripples of the desert.

4
Riding the Tiger

An English rose. The national emblem of England. The pink glow of the cheeks in health. Blooming Blushing Bright. But there are other roses. The rose of Jericho, of North Africa and Syria that curls into a ball in drought, the rose of Sharon that was probably a narcissus. The rose that covers the eyes of a corpse and the rosewater that scents lovers and sweetmeats.

Today Gregory told me on the telephone that he had AIDS. We could both hear each other's TV, 60 miles between us, words like 'Saudi Arabia' and 'The Allied Forces', and someone was knocking on Greg's door. 'Anyway,' he says, 'have a good holiday. Where are you going?'

J.K. walks through a 'BeachPark' built on volcanic rubble; swimming pool and pizza malls and discos by the pool and there's nothing else but creaking palms planted alongside white holiday bunkers, curve of beach and desperate sunset. Somewhere else, charismatic missiles glide above skyscrapers. The dark incense of burning date palms and eucalyptus trees fills the desert. Young boys in the uniforms of North America and Europe sleepwalk through the bones of abandoned cattle, unsettling stars, scorpions and a sun that makes them shiver and burn at the same time. Sand in their eyes, they circle oil wells, delirious under that enormous sky, while men older than themselves, also in uniform, murmur strategies, statistics, geographies, parables into their sleepy heads, make jokes, hand out sachets of ketchup and arrange funerals.

'It's all complex on this island,' says the supermarket senora as J.K., shipwrecked and solo, pays 340 pesetas for chorizo and bus timetables.

'What kind of place do you want?'

The words make her sad and nervous. She walks back to the English boys eating pizza at the complex. They stare at her, call out to her, throw rings of pepperoni and black olives at her as she ties the red ribbons of her espadrilles, maps and timetables open on her lap, and she, thinking about what kind of place she wants to be in, puts on her spectacles and stares back. She stares into their pale blue eyes, growing blonder and blonder in the sun (Malcolm X called them devils) and what she sees is struggling mothers, absent fathers, broken park benches under sagging grey skies, poor food eaten in small rooms, places she doesn't want to be in, places she has run away from in search of an imagined place, a place that is not this place, a place that is not that place, a place that is – a place that, like the words War and Peace, is perhaps just an idea. This is a very blue sky. Thin cats hiss into it. Cacti lament under it. Their golden spines shiver in the wind, and from the largest, most formidable of all, another scenario of struggle emerges.

From its prickly heart, to the soft waves not of the ocean, but of Muzak piped from the local boutique, Leon Trotsky emerges, shirt sleeves rolled up, tattered straw hat askew on his thinning hair. He says, 'Yes, I was indeed architect of an alternative world. But I was banished before I could make it. On the run. Carrying it with me. Heavy luggage, my dear, for a man who had to be nimble on his feet.' He considers the cactus next to him, prods it, takes out a small sharp blade and cuts a piece of its flesh. 'I grew very fond of cacti when I was in exile in Mexico. However, I missed the inspiration of heavy overcoats and I have always thought better in a fur hat.' He digs his hands into the black rubble. 'No good for potatoes. Yes I am the same Leon Trotsky who once wrote impromptu speeches on napkins in Moscow restaurants. In exile I felt the loss of newspapers very badly. But cacti suit my choleric temperament and, like me, they survive in harsh climates.' He smiles at a pale woman with straw-coloured hair and a T-shirt with ZAP POW MY WAY sprawled over her pastel breasts. She appears not to see him but her lips mouth the words CAR HIRE to some imaginary companion. 'Her nose is too short,' Trotsky observes. 'I like women with large noses who nonchalantly cross their legs.'

He stares at J.K., whose fingers are tangled in the red ribbons of her shoes. She sits on her unpacked bags, passport in her back pocket, counting pesetas. Trotsky screws up his eyes. 'Let us place you,' he says. 'You who are discontented, I can tell from the curl of your lips.' He looks around him, up at the sky, and then at his blackened fingernails. 'Why do you think you feel discontent more than those English boys eating Pizza Americano who will later get drunk and vomit in the swimming pool? Do you think they don't know they are poor, miserable and needy? I was once an electrifier of weakening armies made up of just such boys.' He stops. Wheezes. Kicks the cat under his old brown leather boots.

'In the Middle Ages, these islands were visited only in the imagination. It took the map-maker Angelino Dulcert to record the actual sighting of the island and the humanist Boccaccio to describe his voyage of discovery in whatever ink and metaphor was available in 1341. Gold hunters and imperialists followed, and of course with all imperialists, slaves. 'You see,' says Trotsky, 'the island proved to be the most significant of the Atlantic archipelagos because the wind system linked them to the new world.'

He gestures towards the BeachPark Development where young couples carry plastic bags full of lager to their bunkers. 'I'd like a beer myself. A beer and my arms round my babe.' After a long silence he continues. 'We will jump six centuries or so . . . where were we, 1341, let us consider 1936. Let us make it summer. Dust winds blow from the Sahara. Hungry goats scavenge for food. There is a drought and the wells have dried. A paunchy little man called Franco, once commander-in-chief of the Spanish army, meets up in the woods of La Esperanza in Tenerife with a few discontented officers. They promise to give him command of Spain's best troops, tough lean Moroccan mercenaries. They walk to a hotel – the patron is a sympathetic English man – and by the time they have finished their omelette and sherry, they have given him the Foreign Legion as well. By 20 July the islands are in Franco's hands and he thus begins to conduct his ideological orchestra with machine-guns. Within hours, in the terrible heat of that summer, trade unionists, teachers, left-wing politicians, writers and artists are imprisoned or murdered.' He stops. 'I'd like to shag that girl over there, blonde with muscles in her thighs.' He watches an English boy stick his tongue into her ear. 'Amorous vertigo in one of these BeachPark bunkers would really cheer me up.' He scratches his balls. 'I am undone. My hopes have beggared me.' Head bowed, he examines a small hole in his cuff. 'Just thought I'd give you some information,' Trotsky wheezes, 'it probably wasn't in the brochure, and by the way, I recommend the local banana.'

The virus is making sorties into my body. Today I coughed up green mucus into a bucket on my lap. My masseur, an East End boy called Spud, says when he massages me he can see another body floating above me, and that's the body he works on. He calls us Gregory One and Gregory Two.

And from the shivering centre of another volcanic cactus, transplanted from some other place, perhaps a happier place, into sunshine and shadow, into the gentle Muzak of the BeachPark, someone else emerges. Vladimir Ilych Lenin. Ripped down from the bloodstained boulevards of Eastern Europe by his discontented children, Vladimir Ilych, great orator with gimlet eyes, now a little shaky, blinks. He is not used to sunlight. He prefers burying his hands in his wife's mother's fur muff. Wiping the sweat from his brow with a handkerchief he says, 'The great sculptor Aronson was enraptured with my skull. He told me

I resembled Socrates.' He smiles, bends down and cradles a small striped cat to his breast. 'Aronson told me, hands deep in the clay, that light emanated from my forehead, but my eyes glittering with irony and intelligence were not as protuberant as Socrates' eyes.' The cat purrs in his arms, its small paw catching his beard, and Vladimir, laughing, nudges it under the chin.

'My political wife, Nadia, she loved my brain, but my lovers liked my lips. Thick lips that give me a Tartar look. While I listened to Beethoven's *Appassionata*, played with kittens, read novels on couches, Turgenev my favourite but sometimes a little Hegel and Kant to keep me on my toes, nibbled cucumbers and made plans to hunt wild duck in autumn, I knew I could play my life in this way: admired for my lips, eat excellent goulash cooked by my faithful wife, enjoy lazy long games of chess, liaisons with admiring and full-breasted comrades, and write the odd book. I spent childhood summers in Kokushinkon reading Pushkin while my brother Sasha read *Das Kapital* – bought under the counter from a small second-hand book dealer. But I knew my destiny lay elsewhere! I would have to fight the seduction of Ludwig's *Appassionata* and ride the Russian Tiger.'

The cat, entranced by Vladimir Ilych, falls into warm contented sleep.

'The day I sat my examination papers on Pushkin, the tsar sent my brother to the gallows. My mother's hair turned completely white and my sister Olga took to fainting at school . . . but I passed my exams brilliantly!' He stops, eyes settling on her chorizo, and asks how much it cost. 'And how many choices of sausage? Five? Yes, the people, they like to have a choice of sausage. The sum of my life's work undone by sausage. Remove it immediately, it offends me. To be deposed by a pig is not good for the morale.'

Vladimir continues. 'My brother, Sasha, argued that any phil-istine can theorize, but the revolutionary has to fight. The trouble with intellectuals is they are physically weak. They finish a debate, not because they have resolved something, but because they are tired. Stamina Stamina Stamina. Just raising his hand in a meeting is enough to make an intellectual die of exhaustion.' Stamina Stamina Stamina, the black volcanic rocks echo. 'Very big prac-tical demands were made of the workers, but the intellectuals, they just want to screw each other and eat long lunches in cafés. It's the same the world over.' He stops again. 'There is something a little frivolous about the way you do your hair,' he says in a steely voice. 'I think you are under the influence of red wine when you should be under the influence of the workers' movement.' His mouth suddenly crumples and his small black eyes go moist. 'I HAD A DOG CALLED ZHENKA!' he screams to the sky. Zhenka Zhenka Zhenka, the black rocks wail. 'At twenty my brother Sasha pawned his gold medal to obtain nitric acid from Vilna, second-hand revolvers that did not fire, and explosives that were too weak. He died on the gallows because he engaged in political activity before he had clarified the principles on which it should be based. It is I who created the framework for well-elaborated principles. I had to put away my Pushkin and learn statistics. To cut the flesh and find the bone, lay in bare detail the economic connection between towns and villages, light and heavy industry, the working class and peasantry. What is that smell?' His nose twitches. 'Aaaah. It is your suntan oil.' He writes something down in a little notebook: 'What is the brand? Coconut with Vitamin F? Tested under Dermatological Control? Getest onder dermatologisch TOEZICHT!' Zicht Zicht Zicht. Seagulls cry above his furious head. Vladimir wipes his brow again and stuffs the handkerchief back into his breast pocket. 'I, Vladimir Ilych, wrote 'The Development of Capitalism' in prison . . . FACTOR FIFTEEN WATERPROOF . . .' the words seem to send him into despair. This time he howls. Proof Proof Proof, the black rocks howl back, and someone dives into the swimming pool. 'I wrote it for you . . . for them.' His hands gesture towards the pool which is now full of vomit and lager cans. He sighs, tickles the kitten's ears with his thumb, silent as he watches the English boys try to drown each other. He points his forefinger at J.K. 'Take your bags and leave at once. Tolstoy said when one travels, the first part of the journey is spent thinking about what one has left behind. The second half is spent anticipating what lies ahead.'

On a bus at the volcanic crossroads, away from the BeachPark, the bored driver plays with the buttons of his starched blue shirt. He says, you must go to Morro J, lays out his hand to conjure something beautiful for her there, and J.K. gives him her tortoiseshell fountain pen which he turns over in his hand, writes slowly in elaborate italics two words, *Pensione Omray*, and starts the empty bus. They're driving through desert dune to Puerto Rio for her bus connection, one hour to wait, three bags, two of books, one of clothes, Smith Corona 1936 typewriter in a pillowcase. He drops her at a small industrial port at the bottom of the hill, the sea whirling gases, a church, a cigarette kiosk, a local newspaper which has oil-drenched Gulf birds on its cover: *Catastrofe eco-logica en El Golfo, contaminada por el crudo bombeado al mar*; and somewhere a ship's hooter shrieks while men gamble on the pavement. What is it, this blood that leaks from her mouth every day? Dark and morbid in the basin? Two red stars burn in J.K.'s cheeks. At the café by the bus station, small yellow butterflies knock against her bare arms.

'Spit it out.'

J.K. looks up into the eyes of a young black woman who takes out a tissue and says again, 'Spit it out.' The woman's daughter kicks her chair with her sandals and stares curiously at her. 'It's all right,' her mother says. 'It's all right to spit.' She calls out for some beers and an ice-cream for her daughter. A parrot cracking seeds on a perch nearby lifts its head and makes the sound 'Hooo Hoooo'. The daughter, shy, whispers 'Hoo' back and then looks away. 'Hoo,' the parrot calls to her, and despite herself, a little louder this time, her lips return, 'Hooo,' and then she hides her face in her arms.

'It's all right,' the woman says again.

'What's all right?' J.K. also hides her eyes.

'Nothing's all right,' the woman says, and they all watch the parrot.

'Last year I woke up feeling weird. I could hear birds singing, my body was warm, my fingers tingling and I was in the Promised Land! So I took a chair outside, outside my estate that is, and fell into the garbage. Yes, you might laugh now, but I could taste milk and honey in my mouth! The allotment was rustling with sugar cane! I reached out towards the cane and cut my hands on glass, my head was spinning and I walked the streets until I came to this synagogue and I ran inside it. There's a service going on and I shout UNITE! Everything stops and I shout again UNITE UNITE, so they called the police. Bloody Jews. I didn't say Fuck you, I said Unite.' She gives J.K. a tissue. 'That's better,' she says. 'Spit some more.'

'Hooo.'

'Hoooo,' her daughter begins, and then stops herself.

She sticks her tongue into the ice-cream and looks up at her mother.

'So the police put me in a cell, and in the cell are a lot of blue blankets and blue was the colour of peace to me. So I thought, if I put these blankets up on the wall and over the door it's all going to be OK. But then they open the door and say they're taking me to the hospital. So I say, 'You'll have to drag me there. I'm not finished with these blankets yet.' And I sit on the blue blanket like it's a magic carpet and the police are pulling it, two on each end and me in the middle shouting UNITE UNITE, and they lash my arms behind my back and I end up in the hospital.'

'Hooo.'

'So nothing's all right is it?' Her finger prods J.K.'s hot arm.

A fat man sleeping on his guitar wakes up. He orders a plate of potatoes and chilli sauce, twisting the heavy ring on his fat finger round and round. He smiles at the child, teeth small brown stumps, and points to the parrot. 'Lauro,' he says and throws her one of his potatoes.

'A doctor in a white coat comes up to me and I knew I'd met him before somewhere. In a concentration camp, or he sold me as a slave, or he massacred my mother or deported my father or lynched my brother. I knew that man. I knew he was evil and could hurt me. So I screamed. That scream frightened me more than it frightened the doctor . . . I didn't know I had so much fear in me . . . and then I saw this woman, this black woman wheeling a trolley of tea, and she says, 'You're frettin' darling.' So I threw myself on her and stuck there like a leech and wouldn't let go and she walked around giving patients tea with me stuck to her, telling the doctors it was ALL RIGHT I was stuck to her.'

'And I was lost,' her daughter suddenly says.

'She bloody well was. But not as lost as her mother. They put this needle in my arse like I'm some kind of rhino . . . there was so much sleeping sickness in that injection I slept for three days. And then early one morning there's someone tapping my cheeks and I try to wake up . . . it's the tea trolley woman. She's got my clothes in a plastic bag and she's saying, 'Get out of here. Get dressed and run for your life out of this hospital.' And I see her eyes, they wake me up, I see too much in her bloody eyes, I see my own mother in her eyes and I get dressed and run for my life.'

'And I was lost,' her daughter says again.

'But I found you, didn't I?'

'Yes.' She hides her eyes again.

'So nothing's all right. Except I'm telling you this tale in the sunshine drinking a beer, and not in a nightie in Ward Two.' She points to a bus revving its engine. 'That's yours.'

Now she is rolling through mountains and red dust oases, beer and blood in her mouth, waving to the woman and her daughter. The fat man stretches out his arms and shouts, 'If you want my body you can have it!' The shape of the letters L and M cut into the sky, as if on a convict's cheek. L for lire, loony, Levi's, love. M for massacre, mint, molotov. J.K. spreads her hands over her lungs, palms warm and still, as if one part of the body can be sick and another heal it. She looks again at the scrap of paper. *Pensione Omray*. The bus shudders and stops. People get on carrying parcels wrapped in newspaper and string. Across the road an old woman thins out her tomato plants. On and on, from the North of the island to the South, herds of white goats and urban bunker developments, on past beaches of black sand, allotments growing tomatoes, solitary cafés, abandoned petrol stations and beat-up cars on the edge of crumbling cliffs.

Canaries twitter in small iron cages. Their master and tormentor, Omray, sweeps the floors of his *pensione*. Cigarette in his mouth, plastic sandals on his feet, he hums an old Elvis tune, soiled newspaper tucked into the pocket of his grey trousers. The jacket hangs over a chair at reception. He stands his broom against the wall and J.K. follows him to the chair, which he formally sits on, stares at her, lights another cigarette, asks for her passport which he flicks through, yellow fingernails tracing the outline of visas and the outline of her chin in the small photograph. His fingers move from Warsaw to her cheekbones, across Washington to her lips, eyes travelling over her luggage, especially the 1936 Corona in the pillowcase. Tired from his interrogation, he leans back in his chair and says, 'E-d-m-o-n-t-o-n.' The canaries beat their wings against the bars of their cages. 'When I am in England, I live on the edge of London. Dog's arse E-d-m-o-n-t-o-n. I prefer to live on the edge of life.'

He asks for some cash, counts it, locks it in a little steel box which he puts into a drawer, locks the drawer, and slowly, slowly, a smile parts his lips. 'Love me Tender, Love me True.' His keys jangle as he shows her a room with a little desk, an iron bed with a picture of a white horse above it. 'Chinese,' he says, and points to the shower which he walks lazily towards, swishing a plastic curtain around it with a magnificent gesture: proud host, Omray, penned by a bus driver in italic ink, brought into being one Sunday morning at the crossroads. She has journeyed to him and his canaries who scream through the walls, and he, one hand tucked into the top of his trousers, screams back until they fall silent, sighs, smiles, reaches deep into his pocket and gives her a small yellow feather. 'Souvenir,' he says and closes the door very quietly, as if nervous he will awake the distressed birds.

J.K. wades into the thrash of the waves, deeper and deeper until she is floating with the gulls, looking out at the European couples walking the coastline. A sudden gust of wind blows white sand into their faces. For a moment, disorientated, the Europeans walk in zigzags across the dunes, displaced and dizzy, fists in their eyes.

A group of elderly Germans sits at a café, chairs arranged in a circle around the table, laughing and slapping their thighs. The oldest man of all, huge paunch hanging over his trousers, suddenly begins to choke, coughing and spluttering until water streams from his pale blue eyes and his steely spectacles fall to the ground. The more he chokes the more his friends laugh, clinking brandies and pointing to him, until, just as it seems he is going to breathe his last, he spits out, inch by inch, a long silver chain, pulling it from his throat with fat hands, mouth opening wider and wider as he pulls out a round silver watch. His wife claps her hands and roars, 'That was a good one! Better than the one you did in Munich,' and orders more brandies from the bewildered waiter. One of the men turns to J.K. and shouts, 'Why are you here?' The man who has just choked up the watch says, 'She's here to make her dreams come true.'

J.K. turns away from their pink smiling faces, her own face suddenly damp with tears. Why am I here? An Englishman sitting opposite her peels a boiled egg. He slams his eyelids down, blond lashes fluttering in some private excitement of his own.

As my body gets weaker, the things I most think about are pain and money. Perhaps my other body thinks about beauty and grace and how to measure value, but this one, my sweet, still has the same sort of fears people had in the Iron Age. Fear of the dark and certain kinds of animals. Things lurking under the sea, under my bed, inside my skin.

'In Beijing,' says the Englishman, 'the government had all the dogs shot.' He chews his egg slowly. 'I once shot my dog. She was called Ogre and I hated the way she looked at me. Too much. It was too much.' His teeth are flecked with egg yolk and he wipes his mouth on an old copy of the *Daily Mail*.

The sun is gentle, the ocean emerald, and somewhere windmills, a reddening creeper, a small garden with table and chair outside overlooking the sea. J.K. wants to sit there. Very badly. But she is not invited. She wants her own table and chair and garden and she hasn't got one. Insurmountable obstacles seem to deny her the possibility of ever claiming them. What does she have to do to get them? Why have some people got them and not her? To have a home is to have a biography. A narrative to refer to in years to come. There is a house in the garden. Turquoise paint peels off the front door which is half open. Sunlight pours through. It is self-possessed, inhabits itself to the stranger's eye with a particular kind of grace, has its own logic and order. Maps of the mind sprawl out and beyond the table and chairs standing in the small garden, spill into imagined scenarios of all kinds, but at this moment J.K. wants them to be part of her map. She wants to be able to point and say: these are the stones I dragged up and planted things between, these are the feathers and shells and cooking pots I collected, this is where I have placed them, this is the room I like most to sleep in, these are the paintings Ebele made for me.

*

How can she make the things she most wants happen? Not in dreams or sculpture or literature, but in bricks and mortar, with soil and seeds and water, in parliament, in the minds and hearts of other people? Who is the citizen sitting with her on those chairs in that garden? What does it mean to be named a citizen? This citizen is prone to violence and that citizen is prone to barbecues in Hertfordshire. This citizen has spent all her historical time surviving, getting wrecked in clubs, murder in her heart, cocaine up her nose, she rises from the eternal, dreary, fetishized flames of her own anger and says to that citizen, so COME ON then, tell me about tolerance, moderation, your neighbourhood, your schools, tact, good manners, tell me about your Gods AND all the wars you fought in. I'll tell you about my neighbourhood, schools, taxis, clothes, ecstasy, drag queens, any number of sad corrugated sunsets AND all the wars I fought in. Tell me about this world and how to be well inside it?

Today Gregory says there are worlds floating in his bloodstream. Sometimes they make him feel beautiful and delirious.

The arrogance of metaphor when facts save people's lives. The succour of metaphor when facts inadequately describe people's lives. The bravado of T, who wore crazy jewels and made sweet wine from berries growing on the banks of railway lines. Abandoned with her small daughter in a high-rise in Bethnal Green, but growing her up good with fruit and books. And C whose twin sister suicided herself whilst swimming in a river one tearful summer. How she decided not to come up again, to put her head under and disappear, and C forever hallucinating her sister in a yellow dress, drinking coffee, eating bread, saying stupid things like Continental Blend and Yardley – as if the century had taken away her language and all she had left were brand names to describe herself. Her breasts dark circles under the yellow dress as they hoiked her out of the river, eternally hoiking women out of ponds and lakes and oceans. She just wades in and goes under, all furtive and furious in useless protest, hoiked up by some geezer in wellies, leaving her sister to mourn and hate her.

And M who never travelled anywhere, except to the liquor store and back and back again and back and back again, who wrote poems and sent them to her, terse with the fear of humiliation, literary references and cryptic asides. How is it that M, alone and broke, drinking away her intelligence in front of the television, imagines her constituency to be professorial gents in corduroy with Anglo-Saxon beards and wives who sacrificed their lives to nurture the sensitive interpretive twitches of their literary husbands – and she, M, describing her life in language that doesn't fit her, that is to say, adopting the puns, tone and form of those whose lives are cosier than her own: a regular salary, children grown up by someone else – never read the world but a dab hand at sonnets, sonatas, Elizabethan musical instruments and logical reasoned argument.

Mega-star! Mega-star! The Englishman who shot his dog shuffles through the market, chanting, a small jar of Nescafé under his arm. A turkey escapes from its cage and runs towards him, gobbling leaves and flapping its wings against his flip-flops. He kicks it away, making turkey noises in his throat, grabbing feathers and

Deborah Levy

sticking them into his hair. COME ON COME ON COME ON. It runs back to him. YALALALALAYALALALALAYALALA. The only sound that can be heard above his warcry and the writhing turkey are the words THE ALLIED FORCES.

Hurrah! I've got pneumonia. I've been blitzed! I'm a goner! I'm all technology and biology! Half alive, half dead. I'm God. A machine measures my heartbeats. Five drips poke into my body. My mother sent me some tartan socks and a peculiar card saying that when I was born she couldn't decide whether to call me Klaus or Gregory. This coincided with an old friend changing his name from Eric to Gus. When people suddenly out of the blue change their name, I always think they've been visited by strange men in space ships. Out of the blue. Where is the blue? The blue is somewhere. Where are you?

What cultural violence made M's poems so boring? Why did she need the approval of a canon that would never invite her bad-tempered brilliance, politics, poverty and ungainly female form to their dinner table?

Does M exist?
What proof does she have?
When did she become a person?
When did she cease to become a person?
What kind of language is going to (re)create her?

In troubled dreams the white 'Chinese' horse on her hotel wall gallops across J.K.'s stomach and tells her in strange whispers that he will return. His breath is warm and wet, sometimes he speaks in Mandarin, sometimes in Spanish, and he does return, this time to say in strange hieroglyphics made from ice: we return to homelands and find they are a hallucination. We return to our mothers and fathers and find they are not the people we thought they were. We return to our street and find it has been re-named. We return to our cities and find they have been rebuilt. We return to our lovers and find they are elsewhere even when they lie in our bed. We return to our people and find they have been massacred and we were not there to defend them. The redemptive homeland, she is a joker, she runs away bells ringing on her toes, you chase her at your peril because she will appear disguised as something else and you will be chasing her all your life, watching her fickle back turn corners. What are you returning to, J.K.? What is your name, what are your voices, and most importantly, what are your actions? What use is the heart turned inwards? That is a lonely home, it knows each crack in the ceiling and every stain on the carpet. It must gallop outwards into the wilderness and perhaps even die there. Come out to play J.K.

She wakes to find Omray standing above her bed, cigarette glowing in the dark and canaries screaming in the corridor. 'I've bought you some more souvenirs,' he says, and drops a handful of yellow feathers on to her belly. She packs her bags, slams a roll of pesetas into his sleepy grabbing hands and walks out to the bus drivers' bar for churro and cortado, three bags, one Smith Corona 1936 typewriter in a pillowcase, and the breathy syllables of the horse tattooed on her face.

*

A prostitute with bruised elbows sits on a high stool drinking warm milk, a yellow plastic flower about to fall from her thin black hair. She has let her shoes drop to the floor and her ankles nudge each other as she avoids the eye of one particular bus driver who drinks half a pint of lager nearby. J.K. sits next to her, bags by her feet. The prostitute glances at the pillowcase and then at J.K., who smiles as the patron brings her a plate heaped with churro and a small coffee. She likes mornings. The beaches are empty, streets are being cleaned, and people have not yet summoned their meanest selves to pull them through the day. She last ate churro with a lover two years ago in Southern Spain. He dipped the sausage-like thing into hot chocolate and said, 'I love the blue rhinestones in your ears, by the way.' Usually a man of few words, an occasional joke and wry smile, observing her laughter but keeping his own inside him, that morning he talked and talked. Had she seen this and had she read that and what about hiring bicycles and heading off to a village famous for its honey and how brown her legs were getting and how much he liked the cool of marble floors and why did she cry that day in Lisbon and how he painted with coffee as a child in Argentina because his family were poor and could not afford to buy him paint and how his first wife died in a car crash leaving their ten-year-old daughter unable to sleep at night for fear of waking up and no one being alive and how she speaks French, German and Spanish and says she wants justice in three languages, how he planted English yellow flowers, what are they called, daffodils, in two old kettles and, eventually – I love you J.K. – the words spoken for the first time, up to now always avoided, loud and brave over a plate of churro, and J.K., blue rhinestones in her ears, silent, receiving the words and not returning them. She bends down and picks up the yellow plastic flower that has fallen from the prostitute's hair that reminds her of those yellow flowers planted with love so long ago in two old kettles. *Gracias*, the prostitute says, and the pinball machine in the corner whirs in the black pools of her eyes.

Stretched out on a sand dune high above the sea, cheek pressed into the sand, J.K. watches the sun slip bloodily into the purple ocean, radio tuned for news and the sky darkening as hours slip by. Strange voices leak through as she stares out across the horizon, shivering in a thin dress under the stars:

ISRAEL, THE ALLIANCE, SAUDI ARABIA, 2,000 SORTIES, 5,000 CIVILIAN DEATHS, DENYING THE ENEMY AN INFRASTRUCTURE, LIMBS OF WOUNDED CHILDREN AMPUTATED IN CANDLELIGHT, ROCKEYE CLUSTER BOMBS, NEEDLE-SHARP FRAGMENTS

Here, it is night. Cafés by the sea are busy. Hostile fatigued waiters carry trays laden with ice creams and beer and escalopes to bronzed men and women. Local fishermen, shoulders tense, stand against walls flicking worry beads, shuffling sandalled feet, smoking cigarettes, eyes on the ground, listening to the radio. Still and bowed. There are not enough fish in the ocean for that gut appetite. Tonight the Europeans are hungry, they want to be filled up. Fists bigger than local chickens, they complain about hire car firms in between mouthfuls . . . ALLIED FORCES, WE ARE THE

ONLY NATION ON THIS EARTH . . . and J.K., lonesome cheek pressed in the dark, watches their shadowy arms lift glasses and forks like giant ghosts from a world that is too familiar. It is possible, though, that it is she who is the ghost, invisible, disenfranchised, the fragile daughter of colonial wars, one brown hand poking through the belly of Western Europe, the other wrapped around a bottle of malt whisky.

J.K. on a sand dune lit by stars and light from fishing boats on the tremendous ocean.

One winter she ran away to the flat marshland of South East England and lay on the pebble beach in the rain, sea lashing, just lying there for two whole days and nights. Three months later, feeling better, she unpacked her bag full of maps, any maps, ancient maps of China, maps drawn in 1310 by the Byzantine monk Maximos Planudes in response to the writings of astronomer Ptolemy, ink etchings of maps impressed on small clay tablets from Babylonia in 500BC where the universe floats on the sea in the form of a disc. Manuscripts which divided the earth into seven parts of the body: backbone, diaphragm, legs, feet, throat, rectum, head and face. She studied how the vocabulary of form changed with conquest, how the geography of speech and desire have all known invasions, plunderings, struggles and disguises. There in that marshland so bleak she could only look at it in parts, the horizon a long white scar, she thought about the instruments of early science used for surveying, measuring and mapping the world. The lenses, microscopes and telescopes that helped the subject get nearer or further away from her object of study, that led her through unknown worlds to the theatre of the galaxies. The further her mind wandered, the more curious she became about inscribing experience and information: if maps correspond to reality as seen at a particular time, what happens if she observes a number of realities at the same time? The word 'perhaps', which could be a route to possible worlds, but used in a certain way becomes the route to a single conclusion. Unlike the word 'if', which implies the discovery of possible universes, by making them.

Her brother sent her a book. The postwoman asked her to sign for it but she had forgotten her name and didn't know how to tell her. And then she saw J.K. written by her brother's hand on the parcel and copied it letter by letter as if she had just learnt her ABC, and the postwoman was gentle, helping her out, laughing in the right way, so she offered her coffee and for six weeks took sea walks with her, made pancakes with her, let her brush the knots out of her hair, just glad she was there, finding ways to keep her warm, stopping draughts that raged through doors and windows. A loner with intelligent fingers.

Loners are the opposition. Pensive, thoughtful and furious, marooned with stories that need to be spoken out loud and no one to listen, curries to be cooked and no one to taste, days and days of traffic signals to be manoeuvred and no one to congratulate, except other loners: they find each other because like all good maps there are familiar signs that lead the way. The loner who both observes and creates worlds necessarily speaks with many tongues. It is with these tongues that she explores the contours of the centre and the margins, the signs for somewhere and elsewhere and here and now.

J.K. stranded on a sand dune between a war, three bags and one pillowcase.

Rockahulla! Blind. Almost blind. My head is full of dizzy blond Muzak. The kind you get while waiting to be connected on telephones. Oh yes! No Bach chorale for me. My head is full of form. Donald Duck! Mickey Mouse! I've been invaded by an army of Disney pets when I should be at my most profound. Are these my inheritance? Fear of death comes and goes. It's life's the edgy thing. You always wanted a garden, J.K. That's easy. Happy composting. Glorious growth. Glorious everything. What can you see?

J.K. sees the owner of the small sea shack on the cliff; table and chair outside, the table and chair she longs for, cacti and bush of herbs, boat on its side and tottering TV aerial on the tin and tile roof, palms rattling in the cold wind. A woman in a turmeric dress, bare legs and strong shoes waters her plants, looking out to sea while water spills on cacti. Someone comes out of the doorway carrying two bottles of beer, perhaps her mother, silver plait coiled around her brown head, pointing to a thirsty shrub. The turmeric woman is lost in some reverie of her own, ignoring commands to water this and water that, stopping now and again to sip beer or examine the broad leaf of a succulent. How did she come to be there? Who is she? J.K. sees her own mother as observed by herself at five years old, pins in her mouth, French pleating her hair – it must have been early 1960s – watching her dress in the mornings, catching the thrill of her presence in gardens or leaning against a car. When she was J.K.'s age she had three children, had been married twice and was now alone, struggling with debtors demanding money she hadn't got. They would eat bread and apricot jam one two three days, and then on payday, steak, a new sack of oranges to suck in the shade. J.K. barefoot, lying on her stomach peeling oranges. Reading in the long grass. She is frightened and she is ashamed. Sometimes she cries and no one knows. Where is her father? She is nine years old and she knows that sometimes people are tortured. Are grown-ups cruel, then? She looks at them in a new sort of way and when they catch her eye she immediately smiles in case they know she knows they are capable of doing cruel things.

Who is going to love her enough to make her brave?

Her mother wore false eyelashes sometimes and lipstick and listened to classical music, but also blues, drank brandy, smoked cigarettes in a holder which she lost often and they had to search the house top to bottom while she went mad until, victory between their teeth, one of the children would find it and she would kiss them all over, laughing again. J.K. remembers thinking her mother was lovely and beautiful. She was allured to her, pulled to her, zipped the back of dresses for her, wanted her, tried on shoes at the bottom of her wardrobe clandestinely, especially in love with a purple patent pair with straps which seemed to promise a glamorous future, unknown worlds that J.K., five years old, glimpsed as she did up the buckles. Every kiss was a treat, Sundays a treat, tickling the soles of her mother's feet while she read newspapers in the sun, coffee and slacks with zips at the side. Love is no maiden in silk. She is a monster who bellows, ugly and wounded. And her children are ugly and wounded too.

J.K. picks up her bags and resolves to find a place to stay.

In the chapel of the local monastery three monks gather around a painting of the Madonna, one perfect incandescent breast exposed to feed the child in her arms, nipple erect and moist. J.K. sits outside the chapel in the shade of an ancient tree, its trunk marked with three white circles of paint. She closes her eyes.

'Just ships passing in the night.'

The green glassy eyes of the Englishman settle on her breasts. He moves nearer, immaculately manicured fingernails flickering across his trousers. J.K. thinks, yes, I am sitting under a tree marked for death. I must ask the monks something. What is it? Oh yes, when they think about women what do they feel?

'I'm a mega-star,' the Englishman says, puts two fingers to his forehead, shouts 'bang bang' and collapses at her feet.

*

Today Gregory died. Slipped out of this century. A few days earlier he said, here's a picture of us, J.K.: we're talking about places we feel happy in and people we feel happy with, about our ordinary everyday lives and the planning of things to look forward to. God is dead. Long live lager!

'Bang bang.' The Englishman falls on to the crackling leaves by the bench. Every time he makes the sound 'bang bang' in his throat, he dies again, in slow motion, mouth open, miming some terrible agony of his own.

J.K. is looking for a piece of string to tie up her suitcase which has split. Gulls cry above the glittering ocean. Grief is an inflammation. She spits it up bloodily, unhealthily, stupidly. She wants it to go away, but it won't let go. She can taste it and see it and she has to spit it out. Here, the fishermen's nails are crammed with fish-guts, tourists translate menus, and dogs sleep under cars. There, a friend has died, it is a cold winter and trains have stopped running.

Somewhere else, strewn across the desert, corpses, charred limbs, the odd shaving brush, a microwave, a mirror and one broken bottle of rose-scented cologne soaking into ripples of sand.

In Washington the currency is dollars, the bread yeasted, break-fast waffles and maple syrup, coffee filtered and decaffeinated, golf is being played on slopes of green grass and yellow ribbons hung on taxis. In Baghdad, the currency is dinars, the bread

unleavened, breakfast goat's cheese, coffee flavoured with carda-
mom, foreheads scented. Mustansiriya College in the centre is the
oldest university in the world, crops are rice, vegetables, maize,
millet, sugarcane, pulses and dates.

Do we exist?
What proof do we have?
When did we become a people?
When did we stop becoming a people?
What kind of language will (re)create us?
It is possible that classic rules of form and structure do not fit this
experience of existing and not existing at the same time.

J.K. watches a storm rage into the crimson afternoon. The sky is
electric. Rain whips her bare arms and legs. Dustbins are hauled
into the air, caught on the wind's curve. Bags and pillowcase
unpacked for a while, toothbrush, perfume, books, a little pile of
yellow feathers, J.K. knows she too is caught in the wind. She is
Europe's eerie child, and she is part of the storm.

5
Book of the Open Mouth

Rain lashes against car windows. Her favourite dress lies in a heap on the floor covered in candlewax. The white wax against black velvet looks like a fierce livid scar. The scar above her eyebrow makes the shape of a K which is the second letter of her name. J.K. shuts her eyes.

H arrives. They have met once before, briefly, in a train where she felt the brooding and bemused attention of someone staring at the wet black fur of her Russian hat (it had been raining), which she placed on her lap, lightly caressing its fur as the train rattled through the smoke of belching industrial chimneys. When at last he spoke, it was to conjure a picture for her. 'Your hat makes me think of the time I thought I was going to die. I was standing on a jetty. There was a raging wind and a huge wave of white froth seemed to curve above my head. I thought I was drowning. At that moment I looked down and saw a black kitten sleeping on the wooden boards.' He waited for her to say something or ask him something and when she did not he said, 'The white smoke from the chimney reminded me.' J.K. guessed from his voice that he was German, and another image of smoke raging from chimneys presented itself to her.

Now, as he walks through her front door, gift in his hand, he comments on the pleat in the sleeve of her black velvet dress, the books on her shelves and the thick ivory candles flickering in two heavy Ukrainian candleholders. J.K. pours rum into two long-stemmed glasses. She is ill. Flu is streaming through her, a virus, it is the decade of virus, and H, who offers her his handkerchief, is in a maverick mood.

Three days earlier, as she shut her front door, unlit cigarette in one hand, box of matches in the other, and started to walk down the stairs, a short man in his thirties walked up the stairs. They collided and he quickly shoved his hand inside her skirt. In the fight that followed with this stranger on the stone stairway, he somehow manoeuvred her on to his shoulders so that she, still with the matches in her hand, was on top of him, looking down at the frizzy blond curls of his hair. He was struggling with her weight and at the same time running his hand up her thighs. Suddenly she knew what to do. She lit a match and set fire to his hair.

After they have eaten, H turns his chair towards her and says, 'You look like a matador. You would fight small bulls, though. The sort you see running wild in the Camargue.' She lights his cigarette and asks him what his accent is. 'German,' he says. 'I like cold winters.' They drink more rum and she unwraps the gift he has brought her. It is a small packet of wild rice.

'Wars were fought over that rice.' H strokes the grey suede of her shoe. 'In fact it is not rice at all. It is a black seed that grows into aquatic grass in certain parts of North America.' As they dance across the curved room, tasting the rum on each other's lips, her hand pressed into the back of his neck, his hand pressed over her heart, which is beating fast, something salty mingles with the taste of rum. It is her tears, streaming again, and he moves his hand from her heart to her cheek. After a while she says, 'What kind of places would the trains journey through in a united Germany?' His fingers, now wet from her tears, draw a map across her cheek: 'Erfurt–Leipzig–Potsdam–Berlin.'

She lit a match and set fire to his hair. The blond stranger on the stone stairway began to burn, his frizzy hair in flames, the palms of his hands slapping upwards, anywhere, her calves, her knees, still holding on to her, until he got desperate and began to dig his sharp nails into her stomach and finally into her forehead, making the shape of a letter K.

'What shall we do about your flu?' H whispers as they dance into the flickering light of the candles. 'Tell me about Erfurt,' she says. His pale eyes settle on a painting behind her. Two vultures hover over a cream satin slipper, a languid red rose on its buckle. Next to it, a thin bamboo stick pokes out of a pot filled with soil, thin strips of shiny paper, gold, purple, green, glued to it so that if whirled it creates an arc of light and colour. 'In this room you have made yourself a world that pleases you,' he says. 'In Erfurt there is a cathedral. The houses are covered in soot and the air smells of coal smoke. There is also a theatre and . . .' he smiles . . . 'good ice-cream.' She follows his gaze as they dance, reading book titles as if they were new to her, and when they kiss under a small book called *Undocumented Lives: Britain's Unauthorized Migrant Workers* she says, 'Well, I think we should go to bed and drink more rum.' He smiles, sticks his finger into her mouth and says, 'Um . . . you see . . . you are quite lovely, but the thing is I have another involvement and I don't want to lie to her.' They dance in silence, this time his hands in her hair, and she says, 'So tell me about Berlin.'

'Berlin,' he begins, and then stops. 'Berlin is where I was born. Erfurt is where my . . . my . . . companion was born. She comes to Berlin to buy lipstick.'

'And to see you,' J.K. interrupts.

'Yes.' The vultures and satin slipper seem to fascinate his eye. He dances her closer to the image and studies it.

'The bird has a snake in its mouth,' he says.

'Were you standing with her on the jetty when you thought you were drowning?'

'Yes.'

'Why did you say I and not We?' she asks as they dance on and she untangles his hands from her hair, holding on to his hand though, both warm from the rum and he pressing against her velvet hips, ambivalent and desiring, his pale eyes somewhere else.

'Because it was my thought,' he says. 'The white smoke and your black fur hat. The white wave and the black kitten.' He takes his finger out of her mouth and presses it against the scar on her forehead. 'K,' he murmurs. At that moment his elbow nudges the Ukrainian candleholder.

She lit a match and set fire to his hair. At last she managed to jump off his shoulders, calves and forehead bleeding, and ran down the stairs leaving him folded over himself, slapping at his blond head with blistered hands. And then, he spoke.

'And because,' he looks away, 'I want to beam love into you.'

As hot white wax trickles down her black velvet breasts, J.K. sees the packet of wild rice lying on the table, a delicacy, a frivolous gift, and pulls in the following memory:

A woman holds up a queue of impatient (West) Berlin office workers one lunchtime in a supermarket while her groceries are cashed up at the till. At the other end of the supermarket (East) Germans queue for shopping trolleys because a sign tells them to. The shop is crowded with people pushing empty trolleys, a can of beer in one, a box of washing powder in another, two bananas and a can of Pepsi in another. No one can move. There are skid-marks on the lino from the wheels. An old man reads the label of a small carton of cream, broken shoes tapping against the beat of Muzak spilling through the speakers. He puts the cream very carefully into his trolley, walks to the cashpoint, stops, bends down to pick it up and read it again. Eventually the woman turns round to face the office workers who are having to dodge the trolleys squeaking past them. They do not have trolleys. They carry their groceries in their hands and have currency ready to pay and leave.

'I queued for food for twenty years, you can queue for twenty minutes. Look! My mouth is open.'

They shout back at her, call her a White Turk, and she becomes quiet as she takes them in, their perfumes, shoes, briefcases, watches, cufflinks, haircuts, jewellery. 'Are you the new world I've been promised?'

J.K. stares into H's pale eyes.

'It's not a good idea to stick your finger into the mouth of a hungry woman.'

'Who is more predatory . . . the satin slipper with rosebuds on its buckle . . . or the bird above it?' he says pointing to the painting.

And then:

'Tell me how you hurt your forehead?'

His hair was on fire and then his mouth opened and words poured out. 'I gotta plate inside my head. Some cocksucker cracked my head. Only wanted an aspirin. Looking for an aspirin. Need an aspirin. I buried the dead in Bucharest, miss. Threw apples on the graves, six foot under the snow. A HAPPY NEW YEAR IN LIBERTY! If you've not got an aspirin, can you spare a piece of cheese?

'My companion and I are together because we are frightened to be alone.' His fingers search for the zip of her black velvet dress. 'But we are alone. I live half my life pretending I am full up.' Outside, bins topple as drenched city cats search for food.

*

'I am touched,' J.K. says to her mother, Lillian Strauss. 'I am touched by H in every way.'

'Give some more form to the object of your affection,' Lillian Strauss says softly, trying not to smile.

'How do you mean?'

'What's his name?'

'I'll tell you when you're sober.'

Lillian Strauss's hands tighten around her glass of scotch. 'You self-righteous pious little shit.' Her eyes go dim. 'Why do you have to ruin everything?' They sit in silence. Lillian Strauss takes a small sip from her glass and purses her lips. J.K. looks out of the window.

'I enjoyed Gregory's funeral.' Her mother takes another sip.

'Thank you for inviting me. I liked his mother. She said if she'd called him Klaus and not Gregory he might not have got AIDS. She's a bit weird isn't she? We're having supper together on Tuesday.' She looks at her daughter, whose eyes are glued to the window.

'If I'd known I was going to blubber, I would have taken a tissue.' Lillian Strauss stands up. Walks to the sink and pours her drink into it.

'Bloody good stuff to waste,' she says, slamming down the empty glass.

'Mom,' J.K. says.

'Don't call me Mom. And don't ever have children. They'll just end up hating you. That's what happens to parents. Their children hate them.'

*

'Let's have a baby,' H says to J.K. His hand rests on her belly. It is summer. A small aeroplane hums above them. Her camellia has flowered again, another pink bud opening in the petrol winds of the city. She looks around her room; a little saucer full of yellow canary feathers, pebbles, postcards, a bag full of coins, an address book, a white bowl on a stand, a photograph of Gregory, a cashew nut in its shell – not unlike a foetus – a poster of a man with a dragonfly taped to his forehead, a green ribbon, the letters X Y Z scrawled on the back of an envelope in felt pen, a picture of an orange hand with six fingers, ALIEN written underneath it, and a 1936 Smith Corona typewriter. J.K. feels panic rise in her chest. The same panic she always feels when arriving at a new place. She is in a new place. She is in H's arms and the aeroplane nearly drowned out his words, but she heard them and he is waiting for her reply.

This is a frightening place. His hand on her belly. More frightening than walking the city late at night, alone, in clothes that make running away difficult. Than the crazy gaze of bureaucrats in uniform, thin youths with knives, the violent hands of a commuter in pinstripes.

'I hope,' H says, 'that when I touch you, you can feel everything I feel for you.'

Mother. The word is full of pain and rage and love. Her children play in small city parks. Cut their feet on glass. Howl into pillows. That's what children do. They howl into pillows. Howl for justice, for beans, for God, for love.

'I'll think about it.'

After a while he says:

'I'll drive you to the airport.'

She is walking past a cement factory, straw hat on her head, books under her arm. J.K. knows she will have to collect ten 100-peseta coins to phone H from a call box. She knows she will have to find out what the international dialling code is and she will have to find a voice to talk to him with. She could say, why are you there and I'm here? She could say, I'm learning the language, I'm brown and strong, the scar on my forehead is completely gone, every day I dive into the sea and every day is full of you. And then she remembers the eyes of a woman in her early fifties irrigating her garden in Southern Europe, drinking a glass of home-made lemonade at the end of the day after she had scrubbed the soil from her fingernails. What was that look in her eyes? Betrayal. J.K. knew she had been betrayed. Utterly. And the woman knew J.K. knew so she felt humiliated and when their eyes met J.K. had to pretend not to know. She had to find a way of meeting her eye dispossessed of knowledge. What does J.K. know? She knows that no one is innocent. Only the privileged and sentimental can afford to be unknowing.

J.K. is guilty. She buys the black-haired waitress at the local bar a beer and asks her to describe her room and all the things in it. And who do you love? And how do you survive on your wages? And how is your life different from your mother's life? And then, much later, she asks her for some 100-peseta coins for the telephone box.

*

Telefonica-dialling codes:

COLUMBIA 07-57

BRASIL 07-55

EMIRATOS ARABES-UNIDOS 07-971

CHILE 07-38

YUGOSLAVIA 07-38

INDONESIA 07-62

J.K. studies codes. A code is a collection of laws. A system of rules and regulations, of signals and symbols. So now, as she drops the coins into the steel slot of the telephone, she is thinking about rules, signals and symbols. H says, 'Is that you J.K.?'

My precious.
  My sweet.
  My darling.
  My lovely.
  What is German for 'the twentieth century'?
  Das zwanzigste Jahrhundert.
  And how do you say 'enigma'?
  Enigma.

J.K. has two coins left. She rolls them into the slot.
  And how do you say, 'the open mouth'?
  Der offene Mund.

6

Swallowing Geography

She is the wanderer, bum, émigré, refugee, deportee, rambler, strolling player. Sometimes she would like to be a settler, but curiosity, grief and disaffection forbid it. She is however in love with the settler X, he being all that she is not.

Today she found two birds' eggs, pale blue, one in a field and one on the pavement of a city. She buys an envelope in a post office so she can send them to a friend who will appreciate them. The clerk is intrigued that she is wrapping two small cracked bloody eggs in a sheet of white tissue paper and putting them into an envelope. This same envelope will be stamped, inscribed with the name of the place she has posted it from. The receiver will now be able to imagine the sender in that place and make a picture of it in her mind's eye.

The wanderer Y is not without purpose, but the purpose is not wholly revealed. Sometimes she imagines the layout of land before she has actually seen it. Instead of following a map, she has made a map. Sometimes she is visible and sometimes she is invisible. This is not because she is a ghost or a mystic, but because some people want to see her and some people do not. The word absence suggests non-presence, loss, being nowhere, non-appearance, lacking. That's what the Turkish worker on a German tram told her, fanning out his hands for her so she could see the offal under his fingernails. 'This is the liver of a cow,' he said. 'We at the slaughterhouse carry the inner organs of beasts, carry their bodies on bits of our bodies.'

When she meets a stranger and they tell each other stories, she notes that it is always the people she leaves out of the stories that interest the stranger most. If she talks about her brother, sister and father, the stranger wants to know all about her mother. Therefore she learns that absence is often more interesting than presence.

Although she is walking forwards, one foot in front of the other, she is also walking backwards. This is because she is thinking of her past. Beginnings and endings curl into each other like a snake with its tail in its mouth. There was a man who wept and said, 'I can't remember myself. I see and recognize myself in the bodies and voices of other people. I know that we once worshipped in the same temple. I know that the same priests blessed us with basil leaves and water. I know we fought the same revolutions, told the same jokes and went to the same schools. I have been described somewhere but I don't know where to find myself.'

*

The settler X kisses the wanderer Y on lips that are cracked from wind, and says, this is the statue of my local poet, engineer, architect, painter, banker, philanthropist, scientist, mayor, and here, a statue of the local martyr. He takes her by the arm and points; this is my park, my shop, my dentist, doctor and baker. She is eating a burger and chips. Always be ready to eat a burger and chips, a Czech refugee said once, in a television studio. All the while he had a kitten on his lap and he stroked it. He said the cat wandered into the studio and he wanted to be filmed stroking it whilst talking about exile, so it would not seem as if he was in pain.

X and Y make love in her hotel room, the shutter open, a breeze on her left thigh. Someone is jangling keys in the corridor outside, and upstairs someone is singing a pop song. X says, I have to go now. His head is resting on a pillow inscribed with the name of the hotel; blue thread sewn into white cotton.

Is the settler X privileged and the wanderer Y deprived? For X and his partner Z, settled in the country of each other, there is something called a future.

For the deprived there is no word called future.
For the privileged there is only the future.
For the deprived the present is full of the absence of privilege.
For the privileged the present is full of the absence of deprivation.

Or is the wanderer Y privileged? Both intimate and alien, she can touch the world with a phantom hand.

*

X returns home to a chicken cooked by Z. Y eats takeaway pizza on her balcony and washes her hands with a tiny square of perfumed soap inscribed with the hotel's name.

She packs her bag.

Each new journey is a mourning for what has been left behind. The wanderer sometimes tries to recreate what has been left behind, in a new place. This always fails. To muster courage and endurance for a journey, it has to be embarked on with something like ambivalence. To retreat is to wane, fade, shrink, get less. This suggests that the privileged, who are not used to retreating, swell, expand and get more.

X rings through to the hotel and asks Y to stay one more night.

She, the wanderer, bum, refugee and rambler, drinks scotch on the rocks in a long glass, sitting in the corner of a bar. She smokes a cigarette bought in a small kiosk whilst changing trains at the last border she crossed. A border is an undefined margin between two things, sanity and insanity, for example. It is an edge. To be marginal is to be not fully defined. This thought excites her.

Although she is drinking whisky and smoking tobacco in a crowded bar in a strange city, and although she spends most of her time in cities, she often wants to be near water, to be under the stars, to feel the wind on her cheeks and wrists, to collect cones and kernels, shells, fossils, pebbles. She returns to the city with a bag full of these things. When she empties them out on to a carpet or floorboards or the wooden surface of a table, she puts her hand over them and they pulse into her palm. It is then she wonders if these are the things that give her health and special endurance. Some become mementos, some gifts, and the most special become talismans.

So now in the palm of her hand is a small brown feather.

X walks towards her. They drink more whisky. He tells her how glad he is she's stayed on an extra night. He talks and she listens. He says, 'I feel very sad tonight.' In fact she too is feeling sad, but he has not considered that this might be so and tells her a tale. While she is hearing why he is sad, she is also hearing voices from the radio blaring behind the bar. There has been an earthquake somewhere. A man is weeping. He is saying through an interpreter, 'I lost my wife's mother, my four children and my house. They are all gone.' The interpreter describes objects buried in the rubble. X does not hear these voices and he does not hear the unspoken sad voice of Y.

'Let's go for a swim.'

'It's dark,' he says.

'I know.'

He, the settler, present, visible and somewhere, is reluctant to swim with the wanderer at a strange hour. He has a home and he has Z to return to. He will return wet and Z will ask him why. How is he to relate the small intimate moments of his day to his co-settler? 'I drank whisky in a bar with my lover, and then we went for a swim.'

After a while he says, 'I'll watch you.'

While she swims and he watches her, she, like the privileged, will be perceptible, observed, present to the eye, witnessed. What she does not know is that he will watch her swim, and he will make her up. To him at that moment her eyelashes are blue, her wrists jangle with silver bands of alchemy and her hair is oiled with jasmine. In this way he will have stripped her of the possibility of being sad, needing things, having a past, present and future.

The sound of men and women wailing, and interpreters murmuring above them, leaks out of the radio.

They leave the bar. Sweepers in orange jackets clean the gutters. He puts his arm through hers and she strokes it with the small brown feather she has been holding all night. They walk out of town, across a road and then under a small bridge. Swans sleep on the river, necks tucked under their wings, floating silently under the moon.

She takes off her clothes. He watches her some of the time and he watches the swans. She is standing on the muddy bank. She is naked. He is clothed. X the settler has chosen not to swim. Y the wanderer is going to dive into the water and she is going to swim.

'Take off your earrings.'
She gives them to him.
'Don't swallow the water,' he shouts.

She swallows and swallows the water. And as she swallows she swallows the possibility she will always be alone. Swallows the river that will flow into the sea that is made from other waters that have flowed from mountains and hills, that will leak into oceans. She swallows geography, learns to swim in changing tides and temperatures, learns different strokes of the arms and legs, learns to speak in many tongues. She does this because she has no choice but to do so, and she comes out of the river to find him there, holding her earrings in his hand, and he says, 'But they don't fit. Who are you?'

'Who are you?' he said, backing away from the creature that emerged, streaked in mud, speaking a language he did not understand. 'Lie with me a while,' she murmured, and he, entranced by her golden fur drying under the moon, understood the request and consented. They lay together on the river bank while the swans, curved into themselves, slept on, both thinking how odd the fragrance of the other was, the texture of their skin and hair, the way their lips and tongues met, the way their bodies joined together. Both kept trying to find something recognizable, familiar in the other, but they could not. This was frightening but it was also arousing, and they experimented shyly with ways of pleasing each other. All the while he held a pair of earrings in his hand and would not let go. 'Take me to meet your family,' she said, lying on top of him, her golden belly rising and falling. At that moment he lost his desire and tried to separate himself from her, and at that moment the swans swam to the bank of the river to watch them.

'Why do you hate me?' she said, staring into his very blue eyes.

'I don't.'

'You do.'

'I want you to be someone else.'

After a pause, he said again, 'Who are you?'

'I am the stranger who desires you and I have come to convince you it is truly you, in all your particularity, whom I desire.'

This made him sob, great gulping tears that made him ugly, mouth open, face crumpled until he found that he was howling and had to press his face into the mud to stifle his cries.

She said again, 'It is truly you, in all your particularity, whom I desire,' and he looked up into the black snout of her nose, at her golden paws and pink eyes, and vomited, spewed out the contents of his stomach, mostly chicken, into a little pool by his feet.

X wakes up from this short dream to see Y come out of the water, naked, and he says, 'Hi. I've been waiting for you. Here are your earrings.' He gives them to her. The wind blows and her breath tastes of whisky and mud.

As she dries herself Y asks X what he did while she was swimming.

'I watched you swim and then I fell asleep,' he says. And then he tells her he must go because Z will be waiting up for him.

'Stay,' she says.

He is silent.

She knows that by asking him to stay, she has invited him to tell her about his politics, ceremonies, poetry and food. She has broken a rule. She knows that though she has wandered through the country of his person, Z has permanent residence there. She knows this because she, the wanderer, has to know her heart and she has to know his heart. She has broken a rule and she runs the risk of being deported.

'Why do you hate me?' she asks.

'I don't.'

'You do.'

After a while he says, 'I want you to be someone else.'

'Who do you want me to be?'

An hour later, X will sit in front of a log fire with Z.

'Tell me about your day,' he says.

Z runs her fingers through her short-cropped hair and stares into the fire. With her other hand she strokes the cat on her lap. 'Today we got a postcard from B. Look.' She shows him the card, an image of a date palm on the edge of a desert, and in the distance, white thorns.

'It is as if the desert has been posted through our front door,' she says. 'All day I have been tasting and smelling the desert, imagining its light and scale. And when I did my shopping, I imagined B there, sitting on ripples of sand.' She looks at X, her co-settler. 'What did you do today?'

'I went to the office early and left late. Then I came home and ate chicken with you. Then I had a whisky in a bar and went for a walk by the river.' Her hand moves slowly across the cat on her lap. The half moons of her fingernails glisten in its fur. 'Come here,' he says and pulls her towards him. He kisses her eyelids and tickles her neck with a small brown feather.

'You're wearing your hair down,' she says, winding a silver strand round and round her finger. 'I've never seen it loose before. You look like a stranger.' And then she says, 'Why do you hate me?'

'I don't.'

'You do.'

After a while he says, 'I want you to be someone else.'

Z takes the feather from his hand and strokes her wrist. She is feeling homesick, here in her own country, in her own home, in the bosom of her family, with her co-settler X.

Y is wringing water from her hair.

'Who do you want me to be?' she asks.

He shrugs and unwinds the green ribbon from his pony-tail. His hair falls down past his shoulders to his waist. He plaits her wet hair and ties it with the ribbon.

'I'm missing someone I've never met.' He smiles. And then he looks away.

Y puts on her thick wool jacket.

'Who are you anyway?' he asks, watching her put heavy gold hoops into her ears.

'I am a country disguised and made up, offering itself to tourists.'

She gives him her small brown feather.

'Here. A souvenir to take home with you.'

*

She is the wanderer, bum, émigré, refugee, deportee, rambler. But most of all she is the strolling player.

XYZ.

To name someone is to give them a country.
　To give them a country is to give them an address.
　To give them an address is to give them a home.
　To give them a home is to give them a wardrobe.
　To give them a wardrobe is to give them a mirror.

What does Y see in her mirror?

Her hair is wet and it is tied with a green ribbon. She wears golden hoops in her ears. If she is a character, is she dressed for the part? What part is she going to play? Or perhaps she is dressed out of character? Dressed in a way one would not expect her to be. What is going to happen to Y?

The wardrobe with the mirror inside it belongs to the EUROPA HOTEL. Y can see she is shivering in a woollen jacket. If she is a persona, has she adopted a system, constructed a voice to speak through? Is Y a first, second or third person? A first person does the speaking. A second person is spoken to. A third person is spoken about.

What are Y's voices? The telephone rings and the receptionist puts through the call.

*

At this moment Z is re-arranging the furniture in her front room. Her co-settler X is at work. He is in a public place and she is in a private place. So now she is re-arranging the unspoken patterns of their privacy. First she moves the sofa away from the wall and places it by the window. Now she picks up objects that have fallen under the sofa over the years. Coins, a cigarette lighter, a Biro, receipts, buttons, an elastic band, two magazines, bus tickets, keys, shopping lists, and lastly, a piece of paper folded into a neat square. She unfolds it and sees her co-settler's handwriting. He has written down the name of a hotel, the name of a bar, and a time. Z puts this into her pocket. Now she moves the rug from the centre of the room and places it at a diagonal somewhere else. She moves a table, chairs, three pictures, objects that have become so familiar she and her co-settler X have ceased to notice them, and places them somewhere unfamiliar. All the time she finds small things, long-lost and forgotten, out-of-date postage stamps, X's cufflinks, an old lipstick. They have lived a life together and Z collects it like evidence. Her short-cropped black hair is covered in dust. The cat, upset by the re-arranging, runs across the room and back again, looking for places to hide. Z calls out to it. And then B walks in.

X is about to go into a meeting. He is collecting the paperwork he needs with one hand, and speaking on the telephone with the other. A colleague mimes something and points to his watch. X nods. A secretary brings him a cup of coffee. He mimes thank you. Through the glass windows of the open-plan office he can see bodies at work. Sitting, standing, leaning. Another colleague hands him a wad of papers which he flicks through whilst speaking on the telephone, considers this new information, stands up and reaches for his jacket, all the time still speaking on the telephone. Someone knocks on the glass window and tells him to hurry up. This is also mimed.

Mim-e-sis: Imitation. Representation. An ancient farcical play of real life with mimicry. A person's supposed or imagined words.

The person X is speaking to is Y.

Y is in her hotel room, bags packed, speaking on the telephone to X.

X: I've called to say goodbye.
Y: Goodbye.
X: I can't speak here. I'm about to go to a meeting.
Y: Bye then.
X: Don't go without saying goodbye properly.
Y: What does saying goodbye properly mean?
X: Can I call you later?
Y: I won't be here.
X: Where will you be? Give me a telephone number.
Y: Why haven't you asked me that before?
X: Look, I have to go.
Y: Bye then.

Z is carrying an armful of books when she sees B.

'You're moving things,' B says. 'Why?'

Z drops the books on the newly positioned sofa and walks over to her. 'I got a postcard from you yesterday. I can't believe you're here. I thought you were there. I've been imagining you there.'

B is tanned. Her shoulders are smooth and brown. 'I got back three days ago.' She looks around at the front room. 'I've been imagining this room,' she says. 'I knew exactly where the table is, or was. You sat there,' she points, 'and I sat here. But you've changed it.' She smiles. 'It's like waking up on the wrong side of the bed.' She runs her fingers through Z's short hair. 'Oh honey,' she says. They kiss in the disordered room. This is the first time they have kissed. Like that. Slow and long. Z strokes B's bare shoulder and then moves her hand to her breasts.

X is having a drink after work with a male colleague. 'I think I am in love,' he says. 'But I don't want to hurt my wife.'

Y is about to get on a train. She is returning to the city she knows better than other cities. She knows how its transport works, where its most obscure coffee bars are hidden, opening and closing times, its swimming pools, banks, nightclubs, cheap restaurants, theatres and cinemas.

'Oh honey.'
   'You're lovely.'
   'Oh.'
   'There.'
   'That's nice.'
   'Like that?'

'Hmm.'

'Oh.'

'Sweetheart.'

'Hmm.'

'There.'

'Is that nice?'

'Harder.'

'Oh.'

'Oh baby.'

'Oh.'

'Aren't you beautiful?'

X walks in to find his co-settler Z naked in the arms of their co-friend B who at this moment has her head buried between the thighs of Z. In addition this is happening in his front room which has been re-arranged and he does not know where anything is. Nor, it occurs to him, does he know who his co-settler is, how she might want to be touched, or where she wants to live, because he hears these words fall from her lips into the crease of B's brown neck.

'Take me somewhere else.'

Y is lying in a bath in the place she calls her home in the city she knows best. She is listening to music and the kettle is boiling. On the small desk next to her computer, she has placed five white goose feathers in a tin can. Her clothes hang on a rail. Her bed-linen is familiar and cool. Her cupboard is full of spices in labelled glass jars. She knows every book on her shelf. She knows what the view out of her window will be. So now she is lying in her bath looking out of the window and she knows that at about nine o'clock she will meet a friend and they will eat out somewhere in the centre of the city. They will link arms and walk through the traffic as if they have nine lives.

Z looks up into the eyes of her co-settler X.

His hands are in his pockets.

B puts on her T-shirt and smiles at X.

'Hello,' she says. And then she zips up her jeans and asks Z if she has any wine in the house.

'No,' X says.

'Yes,' Z says. She slips her hands into the pocket of her silk blouse, bought with X's money, and gives him the piece of paper folded into a small square she found that morning. X unfolds it. It says HOTEL EUROPA, BAR LEONARDO, 6 P.M.

'Go and find her,' Z says.

B calls out to the cat who is hiding under the table.

After a while, X says, 'I don't know where she is.'

Y is eating pasta in a café in the centre of the city with her friend. It is busy and hot and the tables are full of pimps, lovers, prostitutes, friends, students, tourists and loners reading journals. They stare, talk, fight, shout out for ashtrays, ask for advice, borrow money, joke, cry, tell lies, describe their families, romances, children, and some even tell their companion that they love them.

What does Y possess? She who owns no property, has no inheritance, husband, children, savings or pension plan? Y is a first, second and third person. These are all her voices. X Y Z. Z and X will reconcile their differences, buy things for their home and grow old together. Will Y grow old? Have we met her elderly and survived and occupying public space, not with melancholy or eccentricity, but as a matter of fact?

Y dips her bread in her wine.

'Fear is an invented thing,' she says.

'How do you uninvent it then?' J.K. asks in Spanish.

'You ask too many questions,' Y replies in English.

At that moment B walks in and they invite her to sit at their table.

Don't miss Deborah Levy's other sharp, insightful, and eloquent books:

Swimming Home: A Novel

Shortlisted for the Man Booker Prize

Two families gather at a villa in the hills above Nice. When they arrive, there's a body in the swimming pool. But the girl is very much alive. She walks naked out of the water and into the heart of their holiday.

"Exquisite." —*The New Yorker*

"Readers will have to resist the temptation to hurry up in order to find out what happens . . . Our reward is the enjoyable, if unsettling, experience of being pitched into the deep waters of Levy's wry, accomplished novel."

—Francine Prose, *The New York Times Book Review*

The Unloved: A Novel

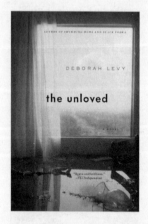

A group of hedonistic international tourists gathers to celebrate
the holidays in a remote French chateau. When a woman is
brutally murdered, the subsequent inquiry into the death proves
to be more of an investigation into the nature of identity, love,
insatiable rage, and sadistic desire.

"Graphic, claustrophobic and fractured, this is emotionally
violent and challenging work from a bold modern writer."
—*Kirkus Reviews*

"Impressively ambitious . . . Unusual and memorable."
—*Times Literary Supplement*

Black Vodka: Ten Stories

"These ominous, odd, erotic stories burrow deep into your brain."
—*Financial Times*

Things I Don't Want to Know: On Writing

A luminescent treatise on writing, love, and loss.

"A profound and vivid little volume that is less about the craft
than the necessity of making literature."
—*Los Angeles Times* Page-Turner blog